Legacies

A Novel
By

Beth Gribas

Cover design idea by: Beth Gribas
Cover design by: Tayler Gribas and Zachary Gribas
Interior design by: Beth Gribas
Printed in the United States of America
Published by: Pine Tree Family Publishing Group
ISBN: 979-8-9988145-3-2
First Edition

"We are the sum of the stories passed down and the love we choose to carry forward - our legacies of love, strength and dedication."

— Legacies

DEDICATION

For my family—
who held space for this story to be written,
and for every memory we've shared and saved,
reflected in glimpses within these pages—
the same, yet different.

To anyone who has grieved the loss of a parent.
To every caregiver who has loved someone through forgetting—
fading away like a drifting cloud.

To anyone who served in the US Military,
and to your families that also made sacrifices
so you could do your duty to protect us.

Preface

The idea for this book came to me one day long ago. I put some words together in a first draft back when phones hung on the kitchen wall and AOL was still dial-up. Then life intervened, and the book was tabled. For many years, the characters slept, biding their time.

As the old adage goes, *to each their own, and in their own time.* And so the characters in this story waited—maturing like a fine wine.

Fast forward to April 2025. Emma and her family, dormant long enough, began to stir. Their story demanded to be heard. And so I listened.

While the characters in this book are fictional, the life I breathed into them came from my own experiences—and from the stories others entrusted to me as they navigated the heartbreak of Alzheimer's. I carefully wove fiction with threads of truth, stitching together a story that I hope will resonate with others.

The poems Emma wrote were poems I actually wrote in my childhood and youth. Some of their stories are taken from my memories but I gave ownership to the characters living within these pages reflecting their own journeys.

A lot of my heart is in this book. I want this to be a story that reflects grief at the loss of a parent, the slow fading of someone we love to an insidious disease that steals them away, one memory at a time. I want to show the hard truths of caregiving—not just its toll on the one who gives care, but on the entire family. Relationships get strained, emotions run rampant. It forces us to look deep inside ourselves. To mend those broken and damaged relationships. To choose to face the challenges head-on or to be swallowed up in loss, depression and heartache. To choose life and the living. To honor our loved ones by carrying on, bringing their legacies forward.

Table of Contents

CHAPTER 1: Packing Up Grief

Emma stood by the window, her cheek pressed against the cool pane of glass. Tears slid down her face - mirrored on the other side by a gentle rain. Staring out at the drizzle, she wondered if things would ever get easier. It was as if the sky wept along with her, releasing its own quiet sorrow. She lifted a finger and absently traced the raindrops as they meandered down the glass.

***

I miss you, Mom, Emma said, sighing heavily. I wish you were still here. I can't believe you're gone. How will I do it without you?

She turned wiping her tears with the back of her hand, surveying the living room. It's chaos. It's disarray. Half open boxes scattered around. She choked back her tears and began packing up her mother's good china she'd gotten in Okinawa a lifetime ago.

How strange and surreal it was, tucking away her parents' belongings. Each item a memory of their endless moves when she was younger. Her dad, Ed, had been career military. Being an Army brat hadn't been easy, but she'd had opportunities to explore other countries and their cultures. Something most kids didn't get. It was nice to get a broader view of the world.1

Focus! she told herself, snapping out of her reverie.

"Hello," said a deep male voice. "Do I know you, dear?"

The elderly man approached Emma, white hair askew from his nap. As he extended his hand to shake hers, she grasped his frail hand in hers and introduced herself - for the eighth time that day.

"It's me... Emma. Your daughter, Daddy."

***

His weathered face looked puzzled, and he drew his bushy, white eyebrows together in deep thought.

"Hmpf, I don't believe I ever had a daughter," he said, shuffling over to his well-worn recliner to click on the television. *Bonanza* flashed on the screen, the sounds of Little Joe and Hoss filling the quiet space. Emma choked up, her sadness intensified by grief of her mother Gracie's passing . Adjusting to being a stranger to her own father, was rough. He still had glimmers of clarity, but more often than not, he couldn't remember her or the rest of her family, *Bonanza*, he could remember.

His behavior had nothing to do with her mother's recent death. Alzheimer's was clouding his mind, confusing him, isolating him – robbing him of his family, his connections to the world. Emma's heart broke at seeing her once vibrant, intelligent, self-reliant, military father reduced to this confused, unknowing old man. Nature could be cruel at times, but …maybe it was a blessing. At least he was spared the grief of the recent illness and death of his beloved wife of 52 years.

Emma grabbed a photo album from the bookcase, thumbing through it slowly. She was procrastinating - she knew - but her heart was so heavy. She longed for the comfort of older, happier memories. There were so many pictures of Emma and her father when she was little. She smiled, her mind reliving the moments captured in the Kodak prints. The scalloped edges curled ever so slightly, straining beneath the plastic sheets meant to preserve them. It warmed her to think of her mother lovingly placing the images there, a visual library of their lives.

Turning a few more pages, her smile faded like the aging photos themselves. She had been the apple of her father's eye – his constant sidekick – she followed him around everywhere, hung on his every word. But something changed in him after he returned from Vietnam. He became more distant, still kind but more reserved - often keeping her at arm's length. She couldn't understand the change.

Her finger lingered on a picture of her sitting on his lap one Christmas, both smiling happily as Gracie snapped the image.

She remembered that Christmas vividly. She'd finally gotten a Barbie doll – the one with the bouffant hair and black and white striped bathing suit.

***

What happened, Daddy? She wondered silently, Had I done something wrong? I know you love me, but something changed after that last tour. You were different.

As the only child, it had fallen to Emma to care for her aging father, stepping into the role of caregiver. She'd left her career behind to care for him. She didn't mind too much. She loved teaching kindergarten – but she loved her father more.

On her mother Gracie's deathbed, Emma promised to keep him home for as long as possible. She was determined to keep that promise.

Emma sighed and placed the album gently in the box on the table, then turned back to the task at hand - packing up her mother's china. She wrapped each plate separately in layers of bubble wrap. She wished she, too, could be bubble wrapped. Something to cushion her from the sharp edge of grief.

With the last of the dishes packed a last, it was time to pick up the twins from school and get them to soccer practice. She'd have to bring Dad along, of course, as he couldn't be left alone.

***

"Dad," she said, "It's time to go to school. Josh and Jenna will be out soon."

Her father replied, "School? I'm late for school"

Emma gently helped him from his recliner and led him to the van. Once she had him snugly fastened in the passenger seat, she planted a quick kiss on his cheek.

"This sure is a fancy school bus," her father said, looking around at the dashboard like it was the cockpit of airliner.

"Yes, sir, it is," she replied, "Brand new. The very best."

Emma started the engine. Ed stared out the window, then chuckled to himself.

"I remember once," he said, his voice laced with amusement, "Back in third grade, I had a crush on a little blonde girl named 'Becca. Cutest thing you ever saw. But she was scared of bugs and all that."

Emma glanced over, smiling. "Uh, oh. I'm almost afraid to ask what you did."

"So, me and Reggie got this bright idea to put a lizard in her lunch box - one of those old metal ones, you know, with the cartoons on the side?"

He paused a moment, his brows drawing together in concentration, struggling to hold the memory.

"Woo wee," he said, "You should've seen her jump! Her scream echoed all over the lunchroom! I laughed so hard I 'bout peed my pants!"

Emma laughed. "Well, did you get the girl?"

"Nope, didn't get the girl after that prank."

Ed chuckled, "It was worth it, though."

"Any more stories, Dad?"

Ed thought for a moment, tapping the armrest.

"Yeah, this other time, tenth grade, I think it was. We had this substitute teacher - Mr. Wiggins. Poor guy never stood a chance with me and Reggie. We were quite the duo."

"What did you two do? I'm dying to know!"

"Well," Ed said, amused with himself, "Old man Wiggins was as mean as a snake. Uptight kinda guy, you know? Me and Reggie hatched a plan and snuck in before class. Just wanted to liven things up a bit."

"Oh, no! What did you do?"

"Good ol' Wiggins stood up there in front of the chalkboard and pulled down the world map. He was all set for a boring lesson, but then he found our little surprise. We'd taped a centerfold of a scantily glad woman sitting atop a missile. You know - from one of those war time posters."

Emma, burst out laughing,

"Dad, you didn't … did you?"

"Oh, yeah. Got in some trouble for that one. You should've seen his face. More detention. Called our parents expecting us to get a whooping. Mom was mortified, and my Pop acted mad. Later, he pulled me aside and laughed. Gave me an 'atta boy!"

They drove on and the memory faded.

Funny, she thought, *He can remember things so clearly from his past yet can't remember his own family*. She let him ramble on as she drove to the high school to get the kids.

Jenna and Josh piled into the backseat of the van and buckled in. The twins acknowledged their grandfather with a warm greeting, but he was silent now, lost in the past. Emma made conversation with the twins as they made their way to soccer practice.

"The big game is this weekend, right?" she asked.

"Yes, and we're going to crush them!" Josh, said.

"They won't know what hit them!" Jenna chimed in.

The twins were on a co-ed team, both excellent players. They practiced twice a week and had games every Saturday. Emma was so proud of them for their dedication. Not only were they seasoned athletes, but they were honor students, too, real team players. Emma tried to make every game, but it was harder now with Dad to look after.

Arriving at the soccer field, the kids sprinted from the van soccer bags over their shoulders.

"Bye, kids! See you at 5:30. Have a good practice," she called to their retreating figures.

CHAPTER 2: It's What Friends Do

Emma pulled away from the curb and headed for Winn-Dixie. She needed to get the weekly grocery shopping done before she picked the twins up again. Her father had become quiet in his seat next to her leaving her a few moments of silence. She pulled into the parking lot.

***

"We're here, Dad." She got out and went around to the passenger side.

As she opened the door and reached in to help with his seat belt, he smacked her hands.

"Who are you? Leave me alone! Leave me alone!"

***

Emma recoiled at his sudden agitation. Frustration and sadness overwhelmed her as tears slid down her cheeks.

She tried to calm him down but only made him angrier. Emma backed up a step or two to give her father some space. She sighed deeply and looked at her watch. If he kept this up much longer, Emma wouldn't have time to get the shopping done before it was time to get the kids.

Just when she was about to give up, George Smithers walked up to her. George was an old friend of her father's that worked as a bagger at Winn-Dixie. He didn't really need the money, but it gave him something to do after his wife died.

***

"Afternoon, Emma. Troubles with your dad again?" he asked gently.

Tears once again welled up in her eyes as she replied,

"Oh, George, he's being combative, and he won't get out of the car."

George winked at her and waved her aside.

"Colonel McAllister, you are needed at the supply depot immediately!" he said as he leaned into the van.

George reached in and undid the seatbelt and took Ed's hand firmly in his.

"Private, do you have the Colonel's supply list?" he barked at Emma as he winked at her once more.

"Sir, yes sir," she said and handed over her shopping list.

Colonel McAllister stood by the van and took the list.

"What seems to be the problem?" he asked in a firm, authoritative voice reminiscent of his Army days.

"Supplies are needed, Sir. You're the only one with authorization to get them."

Ed straightened his posture and headed for the door, list in hand.

Emma took a moment to give George a bear hug and hurried after her father, and they completed the grocery shopping without any more problems.

"George, I don't know how to thank. I was feeling so overwhelmed."

"No worries, Kiddo. Your dad and I go way back – that's what friends do."

***

Shopping completed, Emma loaded her dad back into the van and headed back to the soccer field to pick up the twins just as practice was winding down. They piled into the van, talking excitedly about Saturday's game against their arch-rival.

"Mom, I need new cleats before the game. Can we go to the mall later and get some?" asked Jenna.

Josh reached over the back seat and grabbed a bag of chips out of the grocery bag.

"Josh, you're going to ruin your dinner!" said Emma as she spied him from the rear-view mirror.

"Hey, I'm a growing boy!" he laughed. "I'll still eat dinner, Mom, don't worry. Have you ever seen food go to waste around me?"

She had to admit it, he was right. She smiled and gave up.

***

Emma and the kids carried in the groceries. Ed followed them like a little puppy dog and sat down in her husband's recliner. They hadn't moved his beloved recliner over yet. Settling in to watch TV, Ed dozed off as Emma busied herself with dinner preparations. The twins retreated to their rooms. Emma enjoyed the rare moment of quiet.

CHAPTER 3: A Port in the Storm

Matt, Emma's husband, arrived home from work at 6:30 p.m. He realized on his drive home that lately he was using work as an escape from the chaos at home. He was wrong for that, leaving Emma to deal with it all. He felt ashamed of himself, *It's time I took my place by her side. Em deserves that.* He promised to be more supportive. To help with Ed and the kids. Time to step out of the shadows.

***

"How'd your day go, Babe?" he asked, kissing her on the cheek. "Any problems with your dad?" he said, nodding towards the sleeping man.

"Oh, just more of the same. He gave me some trouble at the grocery store, but George was there to help. She paused taking the green beans off the stove, "I finished packing up the last of Mom's china. I'll bring it home tomorrow. The only other thing left to bring back here is Dad's dresser and that old recliner. It's a mess, but it gives Dad comfort, and that's good enough for me. Do you think you and Josh will be able to help with that this weekend after the game?" she asked, putting dinner on the table. "Salvation Army is sending a truck out in the morning to get the rest of the stuff."

Emma called the twins to dinner and gently woke her father. He was in a good mood. He seemed to enjoy listening to the kids' chatter. He still did not know who they were, though. She had made his favorite dinner - chicken-and-dumplings, comfort food.

"Mom, you're going to take me to the mall to get new cleats tonight, right? Please?" asked Jenna.

Emma sighed quietly - she was drained. She was still adjusting to life without her mother. She had assumed full-time care of her father. And she was still doing all the other things that had to be done to run her home, be a wife and parent the twins.

***

Matt noticed her hesitation and jumped in, "Hey, Josh, how about you and me taking Grandpa down to the marina to look at the boats while the girls go to the mall?"

Josh had other plans, but one look at his dad changed his mind.

"Sure, sounds great!" he replied. "Are you sure, Matt? I know you had meetings all day and …" said Emma before Matt cut off.

***

"Of course, I'm sure, Honey. It'll be relaxing. You and Jenna go have fun at the mall. It's been a longtime since you got to spend time alone with her, with your mom being sick and everything else that's going on."

Emma was relieved she didn't have to take her father to the mall with them, though the guilt of that relief lingered. She loved him deeply, but already the constant 24/7 care he required was beginning to wear her down – physically, emotionally, spiritually.

***

She often marveled at how lucky she was to have Matt. He was her anchor in a storm she hadn't seen coming. Without him, she'd be adrift on a sea of uncertainty with her emotions crashing over her like the waves of an angry ocean threatening to pull her under. She clung to him, or at least tried to, but some days she felt the rope slipping through her hands. Momentarily adrift. Untethered.

She wanted his strength, needed his steady comfort, but she also felt herself pulling away, turning inward to insulate herself. Like her father, she too, was building a wall. It kept her safe, but it also shut him out—and the twins too.

***

This wasn't how she pictured her life at this stage: surrounded by love yet feeling as isolated as if she were alone on a distant shore. Her once-bright self, always cheerful, fun-loving, hopeful—was fading, a watered-down version of herself. She barely recognized herself. In some ways, she felt as lost and confused as her dad. A victim of her own self-isolation. There were still moments of joy, but they slipped by too quickly now, like catching water in her hands.

She missed spending quality time with Jenna. She felt ashamed she had let that slide with everything going on at home. She vowed to change that. To make more of an effort. Jenna deserved that. Hell, she deserved that, too.

***

She promised herself to make the most of this visit to the mall with Jenna, for both their sakes.

CHAPTER 4: Formerly Known As . . .

Jenna didn't talk about it much, but she could feel a shift in herself recently - the way she hesitated before entering a room, unsure of where she fit in. *The Three Musketeers* – she, Emma, and Grandma - had once been a sacred thing.

***

Inside jokes. Long talks. Spontaneous outings. Time spent together just for the sheer joy of it.

It had been special. It had been theirs. A beautiful connection of three generations. She missed those days. She knew Emma did, too.

***

Her mom was so consumed by doctor's appointments, medication schedules, and her own unraveling grief that she hadn't noticed how long it had been since she and Jenna had simply been together.

Jenna stopped reaching out as often, and when she did, her words were cautious, measured. Jenna kept her grief to herself, not wanting to further upset her mom. Less certain of her place in this new family dynamic, she'd learned not to expect too much. Not be too disappointed if things did go the way she hoped.

***

She tried to give her mom space, but sometimes the distance felt as wide as the Grand Canyon. She hoped they could get their relationship back on track. She needed to feel connected.

Jenna hated that grief was stealing her mother from her. Hated that her mom seemed to feel the grief was hers alone. It was Jenna's loss, too. Sometimes she felt Emma had forgotten that, lost in her own grief.

***

Today, though, Jenna was excited to spend time with her mom— just the two of them. It felt rare now, like catching a glimpse of something almost forgotten. But still … she held on to this moment like a gift, no matter how short or quiet it turned out to be.

While Emma went to the restroom, Jenna slipped away to the nearby food court coffee shop. By the time her mom returned, she had her favorite coffee and a *Cinnabon* waiting on the table.

***

Emboldened by the hint of a smile crossing her mother's strained face, she started cracking jokes the way she used to.

"Hey, Mom," she asked, "Do you remember that time Grandma made our Halloween costumes, and we dressed up as Athos, Porthos, and Aramis? That was so cool."

***

"I do! I can still see her sitting at the kitchen table, all those swatches of jewel toned fabric nearly swallowing her up. Reading glasses on the edge of her nose, thimble on her thumb and pins in her mouth."

"Yeah," Jenna sighed deeply, a grin on her face. "She spent hours working on those outfits. But they were the best."

"Grandpa would probably be mad if he knew how much that fabric cost! But, hey, we did win Best Costume Award at the neighborhood get-together."

Jenna took a big bite of her *Cinnabon*, cream cheese icing smearing across her face. Emma reached across and wiped her face with a napkin, just as he had when Jenna was little.

They sipped their coffees in cozy silence.

Jenna was trying to nudge her mom gently, coaxing out that spark—the one that used to light up every room, that used to make everything feel safe and possible. There were flickers sometimes, brief smiles or a soft laugh that told Jenna her mom was still in there - somewhere behind the exhaustion was the mother she knew. Waiting for her world to right itself. To break free of the grief and nearly unbearable responsibilities.

***

And in those moments, Jenna felt a fragile kind of joy, like maybe they hadn't lost everything after all. She vowed to herself to be more help with Grandpa and around the house. Time to step up.

As they strolled back to the van, Jenna felt a flash of bravery. Before she could change her mind, she cleared her throat and spoke.

***

"Hey, Mom," she began, tentatively. " I want you to know I love you. I'm right here. Can we grieve together?"

Emma stopped in the middle of the parking garage, turning to face her daughter. She embraced her so tightly, Jenna could scarcely breathe.

Emma pulled back, grabbing Jenna's hands in hers, shopping bags now at their feet.

"Oh, Jenna! My sweet, sweet daughter. How I love you. I'm sorry I've been so self-absorbed. I've let you down when you needed me most. Forgive me … please. Yes, let's grieve together."

***

Jenna dried her eyes on her sleeve, "Wherever there are two musketeers, there will always be three – only one's a silent partner."

CHAPTER 5: Memories Awash

The marina was quiet, the water glowing softly with the orange hue of the setting sun. Sailboats rocked gently in their slips, their masts ticking melodiously like wind chimes. The three of them walked slowly along the dock until they reached an old Chris-Craft boat, its mahogany hull gleaming in the fading light. They sat on a nearby bench to take in the scene.

Grandpa, who had been silent up to that point, suddenly lit up. In a rare moment of clarity, he leaned in toward Josh and began talking excitedly about the boat his own father had owned when he was a boy.

"My dad had a boat, an old Chris Craft runabout. He kept that red mahogany shined up better than a piece of Momma's furniture. About 21 feet long, I think. He loved that thing so much he named her "*The Other Woman.*"

Matt laughed, "What did you mom think of that name?"

"She was alright with it. Said she didn't mind as long that was *only* other woman. Dad would take me fishing most weekends. Sometimes Momma would come along, too. A few times, we'd take it out to a little slip of land and tie up to the beach and camp out overnight. Catch and clean fish to eat, cooking it over the campfire, roasting marshmallows. I learned to pitch a tent – not as easy in those days, no pop up things that don't need much effort. That was around when I was 10 or 12, I think. Dad died the year after that. Momma had to sell the boat to pay for the funeral. Broke her heart to do that."

Grandpa looked back out at the Christ Craft bobbing gently in the water as the tide came in. Silent once more. Another memory lost at sea.

Matt and Josh, sat beside him silently, grateful for that story – a glimpse in to his past, however brief.

But as quickly as it appeared, the moment passed—fading with the sun. The light dimmed, and Grandpa's expression shifted again. Agitation crept in. His hands fidgeted. His gaze darted.

***

Matt recognized it immediately. Sun downing. He'd read about it. Late-day confusion often came like clockwork in those with Alzheimer's. Gently, he placed a hand on Grandpa's shoulder.

"Let's grab a coffee from the marina shop, huh?" he said, his voice calm and light. Grandpa nodded absently, and they began the slow walk back to the car.

***

The girls were still at the mall, which gave Matt a bit of breathing room. Tired though he was, he took the time to help Grandpa get settled and ready for bed. By the time Emma and Jenna returned, the menfolk were all snuggled on the couch, watching an old black-and-white movie.

The sight stopped Emma in the doorway. Something about it— the soft light, the quiet laughter, Josh curled up next to his grandfather—made her chest tighten in the best way.

Josh had stayed longer than usual, drawn in by that fleeting moment at the marina, the glimpse of the grandfather he remembered.

Emma and Jenna joined them, folding into the quiet warmth of the living room. It wasn't a perfect night. But it was rare. And for now, it felt like enough.

CHAPTER 6: Take a Knee

Emma stretched and rolled out of bed. She paused long enough to glance out the bedroom window to make a quick weather observation. Saturday had dawned bright and clear - a perfect day for the big soccer game. Emma took advantage of the entire family being home and took a leisurely shower. She dressed in navy blue corduroys and a red sweatshirt sporting the name of their team, *The Tigers*. She was looking forward to today's game. She loved fall soccer games and watching her kids play their favorite sport.

Emma and Matt loaded Dad and the twins in the van and headed to the soccer field. She gave the kids a good luck kiss, and they hurried off to join their teammates. Emma was relieved that her father seemed to be in an amicable mood today. Maybe she would get to sit back and enjoy the game after all.

***

She took her dad's hand and made their way over to their side of the field where Matt was already putting up the chairs.

The first half of the game was uneventful as far as her father was concerned, but it was turning out to be quite an exciting game. The teams were pretty evenly matched, and there was a lot of action. Jenna and Josh were really playing hard today. Their team was currently tied with their opponent at the half-time whistle. Ed was beginning to fidget, so Emma decided to take her dad with her to get them something from the snack bar. Hand-in-hand, they strolled to the concession area and stood in line. It seemed that he was really enjoying the surroundings and was busy looking around as the second half of the game started. Emma got distracted as she paid for the snacks and gathered them up. As she turned around to face her dad, she discovered that he had wandered off. Emma thrust her snacks into the hands of the unsuspecting person behind her and began to search frantically. She was both relieved and mortified to find that he had made his way onto the soccer field just as Jenna was about to score a goal.

Emma froze. She did not know what she should do. If she ran towards him, she might startle him and then there was no telling what would happen. If she did nothing, he might get hurt. Suddenly she heard the whistle blow, and the referee told everyone to take a knee. The Ref reached Emma's dad in several quick steps and firmly asked him to leave the playing field. Emma sprinted to her father's side and gently tapped his shoulder.

"Colonel McAllister, your seat to review the troops is right over here. I've been asked to escort you personally, sir," she said.

Her dad turned to face her, and he looked relieved to see her. Well, not *her* really, but the person he *thought* she was. "Let's go, private!" he barked and followed her off the field.

She turned to look at Jenna. Her face was bright red, and she thought there might be tears glinting in her eyes. Josh was looking anywhere but where they were. She knew the twins were embarrassed at the incident; Emma felt awful as she returned to Matt and their seats. She was crying, too, as she sat down in her chair.

***

Matt gave her a look that seemed mixed with pity, frustration and concern.

The game continued, but Emma had lost all enthusiasm. The twins' team beat the competition by two goals. There was much jubilation on the twins' side of the field. Matt suggested that Emma take Dad straight to the van while he collected the kids. Emma agreed. A few minutes later, Matt came back to the van alone.

"Where are the kids? I wanted to congratulate them," asked Emma.

"I told them they could go with the Barnes' to Pizza Hut to celebrate the victory. They'll give them a ride home. The kids didn't want to come over to the van right now, Em. They're embarrassed and upset over the little fiasco after half-time, you know? They'll be over it by the time they get home."

Emma turned her face to look out the window while Matt climbed into the car. The drive home was quiet.

***

Emma got Dad into the house, and he went straight to his room and laid down for a nap. Emma got a cold drink for Matt and herself. "I'm sorry, you know. I had his hand the whole time except when I had to pay for the food. When I turned around, he was gone."

Matt sighed, "I know, Em. The kids know too, - it's just hard for them at this age. They're embarrassed now, but they will get over it. And it will be old news in a day or two. Most of their teammates don't even know it was their grandfather."

CHAPTER 7: Feeling Invisible

Emma waited up for the twins to return home. She felt bad about what happened on the soccer field. She patted the couch and invited Josh to sit down.

Emma could feel the weight of Josh's silence next to her on the couch, like he was holding something back. He avoided eye contact for several minutes, shifting restlessly. Emma gave him space, waiting for him to open up. A few minutes later of silently sitting on the couch, she started a conversation with him.

"Josh?" she asked gently, sitting beside him. "Are you okay?"

He didn't respond immediately. When he finally did, his voice was rough, like he was trying to choke down a lump in his throat. "I'm fine, Mom."

"You're not fine," she said softly. "You were upset today on the field."

Josh turned to look at her, his eyes tired but sharp. "It's just ... embarrassing, Mom. It's not like I don't love Grandpa or anything, but ..." He trailed off, glancing away. "I don't know how to feel about it."

Emma's heart broke for him. She wanted to reach out and tell him that it wasn't his fault—none of it was. But she also knew that he was still a kid, and this was one of those moments that felt bigger than his age.

"I get it," she said quietly. "It's hard. I hate seeing him like this, too."

Josh looked back at her, his face a mixture of frustration and sadness. "I just wish it wasn't like this, you know? He was ... *cool* before. Now he's just ... I don't know ... lost?"

Emma swallowed, trying to hold back her tears. "I know, Sweetheart. I know. We'll get through this. All of us."

Josh nodded, but the anger still flickered in his eyes. Emma sat with him in silence, both trying to understand the weight of what had just happened.

***

When Josh heard his sister vacate the bathroom, he quickly escaped to take a shower. Emma remained on the couch, the imprint of their conversation as deeply etched as Josh's imprint left behind on the cushion beside her. She leaned back, closing her eyes, unsure if she'd helped Josh or added another layer of confusion.

CHAPTER 8: Missing Pieces

Jenna had retreated to her room as soon as they got home, slamming the door behind her. Emma's heart tightened—her daughter was a quiet storm. Emma had seen that look before: the face of someone who needed to process alone.

An hour later, Emma found her in the kitchen, sitting at the counter with a half-empty glass of iced tea. Jenna didn't say anything when Emma entered, but her shoulders were hunched, and there was a tension in the way she held herself.

"Hey," Emma said softly, moving to sit across from her. "You okay?"

Jenna stared at her glass for a long moment before answering her voice small. "I don't know, Mom. It's just ... *embarrassing*."

Emma nodded slowly, her heart sinking. She knew this was coming, but hearing it from Jenna hurt just as much as hearing it from Josh.

"I get it, Sweetie," Emma said quietly. "It's hard when something you love changes so suddenly."

Jenna's eyes flicked up to her mother's face, a flash of vulnerability crossing her features. "I feel bad, Mom. Like I shouldn't be embarrassed. But I am. I just... I don't want people to see him like that."

Emma's chest tightened. "You don't have to be perfect, Jenna. It's okay to feel all those things. It doesn't mean you love him any less. He's still your grandpa."

Jenna was quiet for a long time, then nodded slowly. "I know. But I miss when he knew who we were. I miss that Grandpa. Where'd he go?"

Emma reached out and placed a hand on her daughter's. "I miss him too, honey. Every single day. Some of the pieces are missing – but he's still here."

Jenna didn't look up, but Emma could feel her daughter's hand relax, just a little. She didn't have answers—she wasn't sure there *were* answers—but sometimes just sitting in the pain together was enough.

***

The kitchen settled into silence again, the steady hum of the refrigerator the only sound. Emma stood and began tidying up the counter, giving Jenna space without leaving her alone.

Jenna eventually rose, her hot chocolate forgotten.

I'm gonna go so some homework, Mom," she said gently, brushing past her mom lightly.

CHAPTER 9: Cobwebs on His Mind

The air was different here. He could feel I— he sharpness of the field beneath his shoes, the smell of grass mixed with the distant hint of the ocean. The game was going on. He had been watching, hadn't he? There were voices calling, children running, a sense of movement, but the faces were blurry. Everything felt... *hazy*.

He looked down at his shoes. Heavy boots? No, they were sneakers. *Right, sneakers.* He was supposed to be watching something. But what?

A whistle blew. Was it halftime? The players knelt, their heads down, waiting. He felt the sudden urge to move, but when he tried, his legs didn't work quite right. *Too stiff, too slow.*

Then a voice — *his daughter's voice* — came through the fog, and he turned. She was there, standing next to him. His daughter, Emma. She had the same face as his wife, didn't she? His wife —*where was she?*

"Colonel McAllister," Emma said, but the words sounded far away, like they were coming from another world. "Your seat to review the troops is right over here. I've been asked to escort you personally, sir."

***

He tried to focus on her face, but something was off. It was her. But it wasn't her. She was... too young. No, no, *that's not right.* His mind scrambled, trying to catch up with the present. He blinked, forcing his vision to clear.

She was still there, and there was something comforting about her presence. As he stood, his legs wobbled, and he needed help to stay upright. He barked without thinking. "Let's go, private!" His voice sounded strange—*commanding* even though he didn't quite feel like he had command of anything.

***

She led him away, and he followed. The field behind him blurred into something distant and unimportant. There was something else—something pressing. *What was it?*

The world shifted again, and as they reached the edge of the field, the confusion crept back. He didn't understand what had just happened. Why were they leaving? Was it time to go? Had the game ended?

Suddenly, the *need* to be in charge came rushing back. He was the Colonel, wasn't he? *No, no, that's not me anymore,* he thought bitterly. The nagging emptiness grew. Something wasn't right. His thoughts were moving too fast. The game was important. The children were important. They needed him.

He needed to get back. *No. No, I don't.* Something told him he wasn't supposed to be there.

When they reached their seats once again, his daughter spoke to him, but her words were a blur. He looked at her face, trying to understand. Her eyes were full of something he couldn't name. Was it love? Or pity? He couldn't decide. But it made him feel small.

Not sure how he got there, Ed was home again. The house was quiet, too quiet. The TV played an old movie in the background - the kind of movie he used to watch with Gracie, back when he still *knew* everything. He used to sit in his chair, firm and in control. Now, he was just *sitting*. His body ached, and his mind was tired.

He lay down in his bed, hoping to escape the thoughts that came and went like clouds. His mind kept drifting back to the field, to the children. Why didn't they want him there? Why didn't they *need* him?

He closed his eyes, and the soft murmur of Emma's voice faded away, replaced by flashes—memories of a life he could barely hold onto. Fishing trips. His old boat. The sound of the water, rocking gently as the sun set. For a brief, shining moment, he *remembered.* But then it slipped away, just like everything else.

CHAPTER 10: Broken Connections

Matt retreated to the garage deciding it was a good time to do yard work. Matt yanked the cord to start the lawn mower. It wouldn't start.

Matt yanked the cord again. Nothing. He gritted his teeth and pulled harder. Still nothing. He swore under his breath and shoved it back in the garage.

It wasn't about the damn lawnmower. He leaned against the side of the garage, sweat clinging to his neck, and let his head fall back with a thud against the siding. The sun was high and merciless. The birds were singing, which somehow angered him off more.

***

Inside the house, Emma was with her father. Again. She barely slept anymore. Sometimes he'd wake up at 3 a.m. to find the other side of the bed cold, the light down the hall still on.

Matt had always known Emma was strong. But lately, it felt like she wasn't just strong—she was unreachable. She moved through the days like a soldier on a mission, always three steps ahead, armor polished, heart buried.

He missed her.

He missed the way she used to lean against him on the couch at night, barefoot, hair damp from a shower, laughing at some dumb reality show. He missed the quiet way she'd brush her fingers against his when no one was watching. Now, when their hands touched, it was by accident—reaching for the same medicine bottle or a grocery bag or the remote. And every time, she flinched like she didn't remember who he was.

It wasn't just about her father's illness. It was about loss. The slow kind. The kind that steals someone you love one memory at a time. And it wasn't just Ed they were losing. It was Emma too.

Matt wasn't sure how to fight that.

***

He picked up the wrench and turned it over in his hands. He used to be able to fix things. The broken dryer, the leaky faucet, the kids' scraped knees. Now everything felt too big. The house was quieter, even when it was loud. Jenna slammed doors like it was an Olympic sport. Josh barely interacted with them. And Emma—*his* Emma—had turned to a ghost of herself, hollowed out by caregiving and grief.

Last night, she'd fallen asleep on the couch while writing a list of things to do tomorrow. He lifted it to put it aside but the words at the bottom jumped out at him.

"I must not give in to my emotions, or I feel the wall will crumble; there will be nothing left of me."

Matt quietly sat down next to her and read it three times. Then once more. And something inside him cracked—not in a dramatic way, not with sobs or broken things. Just... a quiet surrender.

That wall hadn't just kept Ed from Emma. It was keeping her from him too. Matt knew now that love wasn't about always being able to fix things. Sometimes it was just about staying. Sitting with someone in their mess and saying, *I'm not going anywhere.*

So that's what he'd do. He gently lifted her head and slid under her, placing her head in his lap. He gently stroked her hair and offered silent comfort. It was all he could do, and he hoped it was enough. *The grass could wait. Love couldn't.*

CHAPTER 11: Downward Spiral

It started with small signs—forgotten words, misplaced items, moments of agitation when things weren't "right." But lately, the outbursts had become harder to ignore. And harder to bear.

It was one of those afternoons when Emma was helping him into his sweater, trying to coax him through the motions of getting dressed, when he suddenly jerked away from her touch.

"Stop! *Stop it!*" he shouted, his eyes wide with panic. "I don't need your help! You think I'm *helpless*, don't you? Just like her..." He muttered the last part under his breath, his hands trembling. Emma's heart clenched, but she tried to stay calm.

"No, Dad. I'm just trying to help. You're not helpless. You're just... confused right now."

But Ed's rage was building, his face reddening as he clenched his fists. "I'm not confused! I know what's happening!" He swiped at the air, as if to push her away. "Get out of my way!"

She took a step back, her throat tight with emotion. She knew that this wasn't *him*—it was the disease, its insidious grasp making him lash out. But it still hurt. And the violence in his words and actions terrified her.

"I'm sorry, Dad," she whispered, her voice breaking as she stepped out of his room, leaving him in his agitation.

***

It was a few days later when Emma found him in the closet.

She was in the laundry room tackling the growing mound of dirty clothes, the weight of the day pressing down on her. The house felt too quiet when she walked back into the living room, and instinctively, she went to check on Ed. Emma could usually hear the TV playing in his room, but the silence in his room was off—*too* still.

She knocked and entered her father's bedroom. She couldn't see him anywhere. Her breath caught in her throat. She looked around again and noticed the double doors of the walk in closet were ajar. Slowly, carefully, she opened the doors.

There he was—Ed, her father, sitting on the floor, hunched over in his underpants, his frail legs tucked under him. His glasses were in his hand, broken. The lenses cracked, one half of the frame bent. He was staring at them as though trying to make sense of the pieces in his hand. His eyes were unfocused, wild with confusion.

"Dad?" she whispered, stepping in cautiously. "What are you doing in here?"

Ed didn't look up at first. Then, slowly, his head turned toward her, and his expression twisted into a mixture of anger and desperation.

"I... I can't find it. My... my uniform. My glasses," he spat, holding up the broken pieces as if they were a treasure he was showing her. "They're broken! You've broken them! What did you do to me?"

Emma's chest tightened. The sight of him, so small and lost, shattered something inside her. This wasn't just forgetfulness anymore—it was real loss. He wasn't just forgetting things. He was seeing threats where there were none. He thought she was the enemy. And there was nothing she could do to stop it.

"Dad, no... it's okay. It's okay," she said, kneeling beside him. Her voice was trembling, but she forced herself to stay calm. "We'll fix your glasses. We'll get you new ones, okay?"

But he wasn't listening. His hands shook violently as he clutched the broken frame, the remnants of his glasses slipping between his fingers. "You don't understand. You don't *get it*! I *need* them."

***

Emma's heart ached for him, for this man who had once been the commanding officer, strong and proud, now reduced to this. His words were scattered and disconnected. She knew, deep down, that there was no way to bring him back from this version of reality.

"Dad," she whispered again, her voice cracking. "I know you need to see, but this is... this is the disease. This is what it's doing to you."

For a moment, Ed looked at her as though he were seeing her for the first time. His eyes softened, but then the anger flared up again.

His voice grew louder, more desperate. “No! You don’t get it! I’m not the one who’s lost! You are!”

Emma’s breath hitched as the words cut through her, but she didn’t argue. Instead, she took a deep breath and gently placed her hand on his, trying to calm him. “I’m not lost, Dad. I’m right here. I’m right here, and I’m going to help you.”

Her words were hollow to her own ears—she wasn’t sure if she was trying to reassure him or herself. But she had no choice. This was the new reality. And she was trapped in it, trying to hold on to the man he once was, even as he slipped further away.

***

Ed suddenly stood up, his agitation evident as he began tossing things off the shelf. Emma jumped back as a banker’s box of old books landed at the edge of her toes, scattering around her. She knelt down to pick them up. The books were actually leather-bound journals – the leather soft, worn and stained from time. She flipped through the yellowing pages with curling edges and noticed the pages were filled with her father’s distinct handwriting.

The journals - so many journals.

Emma quickly gathered them back into the box and set them aside. She would explore them later. Now, to figure out how to calm her dad.

Having spent all his energy in his tantrum, Ed began to settle down.

Emma was able to coax him out of the closet and get him dressed. The rest of the morning was filled with doing laundry, paying bills, cleaning all while keeping a close eye on Ed.

CHAPTER 12: Lost and found

Emma could hear the gentle snoring of her father as he napped in his recliner. She sat cross-legged on his bed across from him with the box of journals beside her. She hesitated at first, stroking the soft, warm leather. The oldest journals were a dark brown – almost black - patinaed with age.

She thumbed through them curiously. She felt a bit voyeuristic reading his private thoughts. Was it wrong to read them? Should she put them back on the shelf? She couldn't help herself. She continued to flip through the journals. The time-worn pages tattooed here and there with coffee stains. She could almost smell the coffee. Her fingers traced the ring from the coffee cup, imagining her dad sitting at his desk, coffee in hand as he wrote down things he couldn't say out loud. This may be my only chance to get a glimpse of who my father really was. She grabbed the journal and began reading a random page.

***

Emma and I went fishing today. I learned just how much she hates worms! She tried to bait the hook but cried when one wriggled in her fingers. She couldn't bear to harm the worm or the fish, so she concocted a story about how she caught the biggest fish, but it got away in the end. She laughed so hard when I agreed to back her up. Her pure, sweet innocent laugh echoed across the lake. Days like this make me forget that fateful day in Vietnam –almost.

Emma blinked, remembering that day – but not like this, with this clarity. She recalled being scared of the worms, worried about hurting them. She remembered making up the fish story. But she didn't remember her father laughing along with her. Or watching her so closely. Her curiosity peaked at the mention of Vietnam. She wondered what event he was referring to. Would she find the answers in his writings?

She closed the journal. Her hands trembled. Was it wrong to read these private moments? They weren't meant for her eyes – or were they? Was this a legacy he was leaving her? A gift, an explanation for the distance she felt growing up.

Curiosity rose in her like a tide, slow and insistent. She picked up another journal. Then another. Bits and pieces of him surfaced. Moments she'd forgotten. A side of her father he'd never allowed her to witness.

The father she remembered was slipping away, one lost memory at a time.

But in these pages, she could find him again and maybe, just maybe, find herself.

CHAPTER 13: I Hope You Dance

Reading her father's journals opened a floodgate of memories for Emma. She remembered the way her parents used to put on an old record and dance around the living room— swaying, twirling, laughing like the world had narrowed to just the two of them. Back then, she thought it was silly. Now, it felt sacred.

She wondered if music might help calm him the next time he grew agitated. It was worth a try.

Once again, Emma ran her fingers along the spine of another journal. The leather was lighter, softer, the corners curled inward as if it had been thumbed through more often.

She opened it to a page marked with a faded receipt tucked between the pages— gas station coffee, day-old sandwiches, and a Snickers. She smiled. That sounded about right.

Emma turned sixteen today. She told me she didn't want a party - just wanted to go for a drive, windows down, music up. We didn't talk much. Just listened to whatever was on the radio. That song by

*LeAnn Womack came on—"**I Hope You Dance**." I didn't say anything, but I was glad it made her quiet. It said everything I couldn't. I hope she knows I love her. I hope she knows just how much I want her to dance..*

Her chest tightened. She remembered that day. The road winding out past the lake, the way the wind tangled in her hair, the music filling the silence between them. She hadn't realized he was listening, or that it meant something to him.

She closed the journal slowly, holding it against her chest.

He had loved her. He just didn't always know how to show it.

***

A few days later, Ed grew fidgety and restless, pacing from room to room, muttering about things long gone. Emma didn't try to stop him right away. Instead, she opened her phone, scrolled through Spotify, and found a song her mother used to love— something slow and swaying from decades ago.

She hit play.

As the first notes filled the room, she reached for his hands. "Dance with me, Dad?"

He blinked at her, confused for just a moment. Then something softened in his face. He took her hands, and just like that, they were dancing— a gentle, merry spin across the living room floor.

He was surprisingly good. Light on his feet, even.

Sometimes he laughed. Sometimes he called her *Gracie*.

She didn't correct him.

Let him revisit those old days, if only for a moment.

She'd hold him there safe and secure.

At least for a while.

CHAPTER 14: Thanksgiving Escape

It was late fall, and Thanksgiving was approaching. This would be Emma's first Thanksgiving without her mother.

The night before Thanksgiving, Emma and Jenna stayed up late, preparing for the holiday dinner. The smell of freshly baked pumpkin pies filled the air as they headed to their rooms. Emma glanced out the window before she crawled in between the covers. Snowflakes drifted down, soft and quiet. She pulled the covers under her chin and spooned in next to Matt, who was already fast asleep and snoring gently.

***

"Emma, Emma! Wake up, Emma!" shouted Matt as he roughly shook her. She sat up, dazed. "What? What's the matter with you, Matt?" she asked irritably.

"I can't find your dad anywhere!"

Panic filled her body as she leaped from beneath the bed covers. "What do you mean you can't find him?" she cried as she ran to his doorway. His bed was a mess the sheet tangled, but no Dad. "Did you look everywhere?" she asked running, anxiously through the house. By this time, Josh and Jenna were awake as well.

"Honey, I got up and went to the kitchen to make some coffee and read the paper," he said shakily. When I got there, I noticed a plate on the table with some pumpkin pie on it. At first, I thought Josh had gotten up in the night and snuck a little pie, but then I noticed a draft coming from the living room. Emma, the door was wide open, and there were footprints in the snow. I think he's wandered off."

All the color drained from Emma's face. She felt light-headed. Jenna grabbed a kitchen chair and made her mother sit down. Josh was already pulling on his boots and coat and heading for the door. Matt was calling the police.

"Jenna, make your mom some strong coffee. Keep her here. I'm going out to help Josh look for Grandpa. The police will be here in a few minutes."

***

The police arrived quickly. Emma and Jenna explained that Dad had Alzheimer's and had apparently wandered off. Officer Barfield left to search while Officer Waller stayed with Emma and Jenna.

Officer Susan Waller, trained to deal with family situations like this, began talking with Emma about her father. Emma explained between sobs,

"Things have been getting worse…his moods are increasingly argumentative, and he's more combative lately."

Emma began to cry again. Her face showed the strains of the past few months. She had lost weight, and sleep was harder to come by. She, too, was quicker to anger, and tears were just as quick to appear.

"I just feel that I am so wrapped up in caring for Dad that I am beginning to lose touch with my children. Matt and I – our relationship …we've grown so distant. I feel guilty for the rift opening up between us, but what else can I do? He's my father, for crying out loud. I'm an only child. I'm responsible for him. I promised my mother on her death bed! I can't betray them."

Officer Waller knelt in front of Emma and gently took her hands in hers. She looked into Emma's troubled eyes and told her, "You need to place your father in a nursing home that is equipped to handle these types of patients. No one, especially your mother, expected you to sacrifice your own health and well-being as well as that of your family." Officer Waller assured her, "Your mother would not want that for you. How could your mother have known things would get so bad? She would understand. Let me leave this list of resources for you."

***

Officer Barfield quickly caught up to Josh and Matt. Together they cruised the neighborhood. Josh spotted him sitting on a park bench. He looked so lost and forlorn sitting there in his flannel pajamas, terrycloth robe and sheepskin-lined house slippers. Matt and Josh jumped from the cruiser and ran to Grandpa. Josh took off his coat and wrapped it around his grandfather. Gently, they lead him to the cruiser.

Emma heard the patrol car pull into the driveway and ran to the door. Matt and Josh were leading Dad into the house. He looked so frail, so old, and so small. Where was the tall, strong father she remembered? Emma opened the door and let them in. She hugged her father and led him to the recliner. Jenna wrapped him in blankets as Officer Waller brought him a cup of hot coffee. Dad was quiet and appeared extremely confused but not combative. He just sat there quietly, looking around the room as if he'd never seen it before. Officer Barfield had radioed for an ambulance to meet them at the house. The paramedics arrived and checked the old gentleman over thoroughly for symptoms of frostbite. They determined that he had probably been outside less than fifteen minutes, and he appeared to have suffered no lasting ill-effects from his adventure.

***

Emma hovered near her father as Jenna and Matt put the turkey into the oven to cook. No one really felt like eating now, but as the aroma of cooking turkey filled the room, their appetites piqued. They all gathered around the dining room table and thanked God for the blessings they had received, most especially for finding Dad.

***

Emma knew that something would have to be done, but like Scarlet O'Hare in *Gone with the Wind*, she would think about that tomorrow.

CHAPTER 15: Calm Before the Storm

Emma knew she had to act before she destroyed all that was precious to her. She walked to her dad's room to check on him. He was still peacefully asleep. She took a blanket from the foot of his bed and carefully tucked it around him in the recliner. She softly, quietly held his hand as she laid it atop the blanket. Leaning down, she placed a gentle, heart-felt kiss to his aged forehead.

***

Her heart ached for him and the trauma he had suffered. He was never diagnosed by the Veteran's Administration as having PTSD, but she was sure he was suffering from it for many years. The wall he'd built also had prevented him from admitting to them – or himself - that he needed help. Pride could be a double-edged sword – providing self-assurance and confidence on one hand and self-neglect and emotional harm on the other.

She walked into the kitchen and grabbed the list of resources Officer Waller had given her days before. It was time to make a change, so she called the respite care number and asked for help.

Within the week, a care agency stepped in to help. One small step towards healing her family, one giant step for healing herself.

***

The first few days of caregiver respite were a revelation to Emma. It felt like a quiet shift, like the sound of a window opening, spilling in a little light, and hope. It wasn't much—just a few hours where someone else could sit with Ed, ensuring he was safe and comfortable. But it was enough. Enough to breathe. Enough to realize she had a life outside of her father's care. For the first time since assuming care of her father, Emma allowed herself to leave the house alone. She felt both guilt and relief at the same time.

That evening, Emma asked Jenna and Josh to keep an eye on Grandpa while she and Matt took a walk around the block. They strolled together in a peaceful, slow pace. Matt reached out to grab her hand quietly, gently giving it a squeeze. He recognized the subtle shift in Emma. He welcomed her attempt to rekindle bonds that have been slipping away over the last year. He didn't want to move too fast, to spoil things before they really even started, so they walked along in silence, allowing the moment to evolve on its own.

***

Later that week, Emma, emboldened by her recent personal revelations, instituted a new routine – one that included the *whole* family. They started having movie nights again, a tradition that had long fallen to the wayside as the demands of caregiving consumed her. But this time, Emma had help. She didn't have to do it alone. Matt watched Ed while she prepared popcorn and settled into the couch, the familiar flicker of the television bringing a sense of normalcy to the house. For a moment, it felt like they had pressed "pause" on all the grief, the fear, and the exhaustion. It felt good. If felt genuine.

She realized, as she sat there watching a comedy with Matt, that her idea of caregiving had always been tied to the belief that it was her sole responsibility—that asking for help meant failure. But now, sitting beside him and laughing at the silly antics on screen, she understood something deeper. Seeking help wasn't a sign of weakness. It was an act of strength, an acknowledgment of her limits, and an act of self-care.

***

She was learning, slowly, that her dad was not her burden alone. And in sharing that load with Matt, the kids, and even the caregivers, she wasn't just taking care of her father. She was taking care of herself. She was taking care of her family. And in that quiet, intimate moment, Emma felt something she hadn't allowed herself to feel in a long time: peace.

CHAPTER 16: Storm Warning

December was edging closer to Christmas, but it didn't hold its usual appeal for Emma – another first holiday without Mom. She was still grieving but had thrown herself into full-time caregiving for her father, giving her little time to work through her grief.

Some days were manageable. Most were not. The rare moments of caregiver relief offered small pockets of air in an otherwise suffocating routine. Her father now needed help with the most basic tasks of self-care. And most days, he met her assistance with resistance. The colonel was increasingly agitated, and Emma took the brunt of it.

***

Emma was cooking dinner as the TV droned in the living room. The Weather Alert sounded sharp and urgent, made Emma look up from the stove, spoon poised mid-air. A major winter storm was on its way: sleet, ice, and heavy snowfall expected by tomorrow evening.

What she didn't know was that another kind of storm was already gathering—one that would crack open the fragile calm she'd managed to create.

The next morning, Emma was dressing her dad for the day when he suddenly took a swing at her, shouting to leave him alone. His closed fist caught her square in the left eye. Pain bloomed, instant, and hot. She stumbled back in shock, landing at Ed's feet. Tears welled in her eyes – tears from pain, sorrow, and some deeper emotion she couldn't name.

***

The strike of his knuckles had been quick and sharp, like the ice-laden branches breaking under pressure. Her vision blurred momentarily, not just from the physical pain. The sting of betrayal –even if she knew he wasn't fully himself. Even though she knew he hadn't meant it.

And then, her mother's voice—quiet but firm—rose in her mind: *Be the calm in the storm, Sweetheart.*

Emma wiped her eyes with the back of her hand and slowly rose. She approached him again, careful and calm, narrating each movement.

"I'm going to help you with your buttons now, okay?"

He didn't resist this time. His expression softened, confusion knitting his brow.

"Your face is bruised, dear lady. Are you okay? Who has done this to you?"

***

Emma's heart twisted. She smiled gently.

"It's okay, sir. I slipped on a rug and hit the doorknob. I'll ice it—it'll be fine."

Outside, the snow was beginning to fall sideways, whipped by wind that howled against the windows. Inside, Emma sat on the floor, her body aching, her eye swelling. Wondering if the walls she'd built could hold much longer against the avalanche of emotions it was holding back. She quietly got up, as Dad settled in his recliner once more. She went to her bathroom and got out her makeup in an attempt to hide the evidence of her injury before her family came home.

***

As she dabbed concealer over the bruised skin, her hand trembled. She remembered her mother's voice—strong, composed, always telling her to be the calm in the storm. But this calm felt like silence, like surrender.

The storm outside picked up, rattling the windows in their frames, as if the house itself was bracing for impact. Emma knew the feeling. The cold outside was nothing compared to the chill creeping into her chest. Her inner voice whispered, *you're breaking*. She wondered how much longer she could hold everything together before she shattered.

Emma felt a flicker of relief as she heard Matt and the twins arrive home safely, but it was short-lived. The fear quickly returned, too.

Time to put on the mask. The invisible one she thought could hide the storm raging inside. So much for sharing the burden of her father's care. She'd try to keep this part to herself. For him. For her. She gave them the same story—the fall, the doorknob. She hoped they bought it. Maybe Matt wouldn't notice after her shower. Maybe the dim bedside lamps would shadow the worst of it.

She couldn't tell the truth. Couldn't risk Matt suggesting long-term care. Couldn't break the promise she made to her mother. She had to hold on. But she could feel it: the delicate balance of her family shifting again.

In the end, they didn't believe her. Not really. But they didn't press—this time.

She exhaled, thinking the moment of dread was over. But one glance at Matt's face told her otherwise. He knew.

Josh and Jenna retreated silently to their rooms, saying nothing. They weren't little kids anymore. They noticed. They just didn't know how to help. And maybe that's what scared her most.

***

CHAPTER 17: One-Time Pass

Emma stood before her bathroom mirror studying her freshly washed face. The swelling was still noticeable and tender. The bruise was obvious now without its cloak of concealer. She brushed her hair absently, staring at the woman in the glass – one she barely recognized

She set the brush down on the counter leaning closer to the mirror. Her skin looked pale, almost translucent. Except for the shiner blooming across her left eye –shades of blue and purple bright against her alabaster skin. New frown lines had etched themselves across her forehead, subtle creases mapping out fatigue and worry. A few new wrinkles. Dull, lifeless and seemingly empty eyes stared back at her.

A shell, a ghost, a flat image of her former vibrant self. Where had she gone? Who was this new person? Could she find her old self again? And if she did . . . would she even recognize her?

Emma stood up straight. Unknowingly, she steeled herself for the battle she felt coming. She opened the bathroom door and entered her bedroom.

***

Matt was there, awake. She had hoped he'd be fast asleep. Quietly, she slid into bed beside him.

He leaned over her, gently, almost reverently - and placed a frozen bag of peas and carrots, wrapped in a dishtowel onto her eye. He held it there.

For a few moments, they lay in silence. Tears slid down Emma's face. She was touched by the thoughtfulness. The tenderness of his touch A touch once so familiar, and now almost seemed foreign. For a few moments, that was enough – just being together in that moment.

It couldn't last. She knew that.

They were going to talk about it.

Matt broke the silence first. His tone was gentle, yet firm.

"Ems," he said softly.

Emma swallowed hard. He hadn't called her by that nickname for a long time.

"You know we have to talk about this, right? I understand why you lied. I get it. I really do, but lying doesn't change the truth."

Emma kept her eyes on the ceiling. Her throat tightened.

Matt slowly exhaled, still holding the ice pack against her face.

"I know you were trying to protect him. And I know you made a promise to your mom." He paused, letting her catch her breath. "But Emma . . . this can't happen again. This isn't what your mom wanted. Hell, it isn't what your dad would have wanted. He would be mortified at his own behavior. It's not who he was, but sadly, it's who he *is* now because of his disease."

He gave her another minute to process. He adjusted the ice pack.

"Emma, I'm not angry," he said quietly. "I'm scared. Scared of what could've happened. Scared that next time, it could be worse. You could have hit your head, been unconscious. What if he strikes out at Josh or Jenna? What then?" He paused again. Refocusing his thoughts, he continued. It's not fair to them. It's not fair to you. It's certainly not fair to your Dad, either. You see that, right?"

Silence greeted him. She couldn't respond just yet, so he continued on.

"I know this isn't what you wanted. I know you take caring for your father seriously and ratting him out seems like a betrayal of that trust. But I need you to hear me when I say this - Your dad wouldn't want this. Your mom wouldn't want this. They wouldn't want you to be hurt out of a sense of loyalty. Your mom made you promise to keep him home *as long as you could.*"

Emma sighed.

"You've done that, Em. Now, we need to explore the alternatives."

She turned slowly towards him, the frozen bag sliding off her face. She grasped his hand. Once again holding tight to her anchor.

"This is your one-time pass," he said. "I'm not walking away. But I need to know you won't let this happen again. If it does . . . if he hurts you again . . . we *have* to move him to a skilled nursing facility. Somewhere safe – for him and for you."

He leaned over and gently kissed her forehead, then wrapped her in his arms.

Emma nodded, ever so slightly. She leaned into his embrace. He felt the tremble of emotion run through her.

"I love you, Em," Matt said quietly, "But I'm not going to sit back and watch you disappear. I'm going to fight for you. Tomorrow we need to sit the twins down and have a serious conversation. They're in this too. They deserve the truth."

CHAPTER 18: No More Secrets

The next morning dawned brightly. The sun was beginning to melt the snow outside. Emma rolled over in bed to find Matt's side empty. It was Christmas Break, so the kids were at home still sleeping as teenagers often do. The house was quiet—almost too quiet. Time to get up and start the day.

Emma got dressed and started to go in the bathroom to put on her concealer. After a moment's hesitation, she changed her mind. If they were going to tell the twins the truth, she would leave the makeup off. Might as well face it head on.

Opening the bedroom door, she padded down the hallway. She found Matt in the kitchen. Pots and pans were scattered around the countertops. The smell of sausage and bacon permeated her senses. Steam rose from the waffle iron. The aroma of coffee drew her closer. Matt, standing at the stove scrambling eggs, greeted her warmly.

"Morning Ems. Did you sleep okay?"

"Surprisingly, I did. This smells wonderful. I didn't realize how hungry I was!" Emma responded.

Her stomach rumbled, and for the first time in days, the scent of food didn't make her nauseous.

"Where are the kids? Still sleeping?" she asked, snagging a slice of toast.

"Yes, they are. Do you mind waking them up for breakfast while I plate everything? Oh, by the way, I called the respite team. They are sending someone over this morning. We need to talk to the twins uninterrupted."

Emma took a deep breath. She dreaded this talk. Matt had made her realize the kids needed to know. It would be hard, but necessary.
"Thanks for thinking of that. You're right. We need to focus on them uninterrupted. What time are they coming by?" she asked quietly.

"They said around 10:30 this morning," he replied. I thought I'd get a jump on breakfast and let you sleep a bit later today. Your dad is awake, dressed and watching *Gunsmoke* again."

She paused and looked back at him. She felt overwhelmed at the small gestures that meant the world to her. "I appreciate that. Thank you," she replied quietly, sincerely.

***

As Emma walked back down the hall to wake the twins, she felt a pang of guilt at Matt having assumed *her* role with her father. She exhaled deeply. She had expected to find the usual morning chaos – shouting, arguing, a lack of cooperation from Dad. It was a welcome surprise. She dared not open his door for fear of igniting a new storm. In fact, she was still a little scared from yesterday. Instead, she pulled out her phone and checked the app for the in-room camera. He was peacefully watching his show, absently picking at the blanket Matt had caringly tucked around him. Dad sure loved that recliner!

Emma and her sleepyheads sat down at the table. Emma noticed Matt set the table using her Mom's china. What a special touch. She saw how hard he was trying. Maybe they could find their way back to each other. It gave her a glimmer of hope.

The morning light streamed in through the bay windows. They devoured the generous breakfast Matt had cooked. They talked. They ate. They laughed over Josh quickly and forcefully stabbing the last sausage patty on the serving platter. Anyone from the outside looking in would see a well-adjusted happy family – if they only knew the truth.

CHAPTER 19: Truth Be Told

Precisely at 10:30 a.m., Donna, Ed's regular care giver, knocked at the door. That was such a relief to Emma. Maybe there would be no drama other than what might unfold in a few minutes with the meeting with the twins. She and the kids headed to the sun room as Matt explained they were having a much-needed family meeting. Emma had opted to avoid Donna, to avoid explaining her swollen, bruised eye. Donna assured Matt that she would keep Ed under close observation. She would do her best to give them the privacy they needed.

The family settled in to the wicker furniture, sinking comfortably into the overstuffed cushions. Jenna and Josh had a good idea of what this impromptu meeting was about. Mom's makeup hadn't concealed anything. Josh stared out the glass enclosure. Patches of snow still dotted the backyard. Ice was dripping from the branches of trees. He could hear the gentle splash as the water formed a puddle beneath it. Jenna fidgeted restlessly, tugging at the sleeves of her sweatshirt. She dreaded what might come from this meeting.

***

Matt took the reins for the moment. Gently guiding the conversation that was as delicate and intricate as the snowflakes that had fallen. While there was some heat in the sunroom, a chill still permeated the room.

"Just to let you know, no one is in trouble. We just need to talk to you both about something important."

Emma met their questioning gaze. A lump formed in her throat. She twisted her hands together absently.

"This isn't easy to say, but I want to be honest with you. About Grandpa."

Jenna asked quietly,

"Is he okay? Did something happen?"

"He's. . . not okay. Not really. You both know he has Alzheimer's. But you may not know just how that affects him. And us. Things have been getting more complicated lately," she continued, Yesterday… something happened," she said absently raising her hand to her left eye. "It's time I was honest with you. I owe you the truth."

Josh and Jenna looked at her, reading her mind.

"He did that to you, didn't he?" nodding his head towards her face.

There was silence for a moment. Emma gathered her thoughts.

"He did, but not the way you might think. I was trying to get him dressed and he got confused, combative. He thought I was someone trying to hurt him. Someone from long ago. He was scared. He lashed out trying to protect himself. I didn't see it coming."

Jenna's eyes were wide, brimming with tears. Her voice trembled with emotion as she blurted out.

"But that's not okay, Mom. He *hit* you!"

Emma tried to keep it together. To help them both understand. To help her own understanding.

"You're right. It's *not* okay, but it was an accident, really. He didn't know who I was. He was frightened. And it scared me, too. I was trying to process it. That's why I lied to you all yesterday. I'm so sorry for that."

Matt took over for Emma to give her a moment to regroup.

"Your mother and I were talking last night. That's why we're making some big decisions now – to keep everyone safe, including Grandpa. You both know the last thing Grandpa would do was hurt any of us."

Another pause. Josh looked back out the windows again. He swallowed hard. He said nothing. He was internalizing.

At last, Josh broke the silence,

"So what…you're gonna send him away now, to rot in some old folks' home?!"

Tears filled both Emma and Jenna's eyes.

"No, not yet. But…we have to start making a backup plan. His agitation and combativeness is getting worse. More frequent. And now, more dangerous. Not just for your mother, but for all of us. We couldn't bear to see one of you hurt. Or Grandpa either," Matt said gently.

"But …you're hurt, Mom", Jenna added.

"Yes, Jenna, I am. But more than that – I'm tired. The kind of tiredness that sleep won't fix. I haven't been the mom you both deserve. Or the wife Dad deserves. I'm being stretched thin. I don't know how much longer I can continue caring for him."

Jenna spoke with conviction if not quite truth, "We're doing okay. We love you, Mom. We get it. I'll help out more. With the housework, with Grandpa. Whatever you need!"

Matt chimed in,

"We aren't doing anything yet. Just planning our next move. Your mom promised Grandma she'd take care of him for as long as she could. She's doing that. But now…she's reaching her limits. It's good, Jenna, that you want to do more to help. We all need to step up. Your mom can't - and shouldn't - deal do this alone. We're family, and that's what families do."

"He doesn't really know us anymore, does he?" asked Josh, picking at a thread in his jeans.

The chill of the air was echoed in their hearts. They all knew the answer. No words were needed.

"We'll take it one day at a time. Let it play out on its own. I promise to be honest going forward," Emma stated with heartfelt conviction. "I know you've all been willing to help sooner, but I haven't let you. I thought I could do it by myself, that it was my duty. But now, I see I was wrong. This is our burden to share."

Matt reached out for Emma's hand, giving it a gentle squeeze. Jenna leaned into her mother, resting her head on Emma's shoulder. Josh sighed heavily and shifted closer to his family. Their knees touching, forming a tight circle of support. The sun rose higher in the sky. Gentle, warming rays of light shone down upon them through the dew dripped glass.

For a moment, they were just a family. Not broken. Not perfect. Just a family trying to stay afloat.

CHAPTER 20: Lost in the Weeds

Josh's bedroom door clicked quietly shut behind him, as if that small sound could silence the voices still echoing in his thoughts. The meeting in the sunroom had been intense. Heavy stuff. Stuff a kid his age shouldn't have to carry - but here he was. Feeling alone in a house full of family. Surrounded by loved ones, but not feeling seen. Or heard. Just… being.

Josh walked toward his closet and pulled down a small treasure chest Grandpa had given him when he was little. He carried it to his bed and tossed it there.

Then he moved to the window, gently pushing the curtains aside. He cracked it open despite the frigid air. He breathed in deeply. The cold hit his face and lungs, but he didn't mind. It matched what he was feeling inside. Numb. Raw. He left the window open a few inches. He pulled the curtains partially shut.

His dim room wrapped him in comfort, like a blanket - offering what little comfort it could offer after the meeting.

He crossed to the bed and grabbed the treasure chest, then settled in to the armchair in the corner. He sat down heavily, leaning back, eyes closed for a moment, trying to still the noise in his head. He used to sit here in this chair and read. Back when things still made sense.

He opened the chest and pulled out the little glass bowl tucked beneath folded keepsakes. He liked the cool feeling of the glass against his fingers. He packed it methodically, fingers moving on autopilot. The lighter flicked, its flame burning brightly in the dim room. A puff, smoke curling through the air, mirroring the thoughts swirling inside him.

He sat there, quiet and still, gazing longingly at the wisps of smoke rising gently in front of him. He wished he felt that free. That unfettered.

He closed his eyes again. The image came unbidden – the mark on his mother's face. A wound that felt deeper than just skin. A wound that may never fully heal. It haunted him.

I guess for mom, it was deeper than that, Josh thought bitterly.

He couldn't imagine how he would feel if his dad had ever hit him.

Another puff. A longer drag. He was trying to chase away the ghosts of the conversation - push them back into the shadows of his mind.

It wasn't working. Not yet. And so he kept gently puffing.

There was a quiet tap on his bedroom door. Josh didn't respond, but the door creaked open anyway. Jenna slid inside, eyes scanning the room. She plopped onto his bed, sitting cross-legged as she did when they were kids playing cards during a storm. She smelled the weed, of course.

"No worries, I won't tell them in - case you were wondering," she told him.

"You might want to light a scented candle or get some air freshener to hid the smell," she continued, absently picking at his bedspread.

Her gaze shifted to the small treasure chest lying open on his lap. Her eyes brightened.

"Is that the one Grandpa gave you for our fifth birthday," she asked softly?

Josh nodded, exhaling slowly. "Yeah."

He thought about how the chest used to smell like Grandpa's garage. Motor oil, saw dust, and WD-40.Now it mostly smelled of weed. That thought made him wince slightly. Like he's erased a sacred memory without meaning to.

Josh reached inside the chest and found the old compass hidden beneath the paraphernalia. He held it up for Jenna to see.

"Remember when he told us this thing could lead us to buried treasure?" as a smile stole across his face.

"Yes! He used to draw us a treasure map to follow. If we were clever enough, we'd find a small treasure he'd buried for us!" she laughed as she answered. She, too, had a smile.

"I keep thinking about that trip we took to the cabin," Jenna said. "The one where he taught us how to fish, and you hooked your shirt instead of the line."

Josh let out a small laugh. "And he told me, 'Well, at least you caught something."

Their smiles faded slowly.

"How did things change so much?" Jenna whispered. "It's like… he's still in there, but *not*." Josh didn't answer right away. He just looked at the compass in her hand.

"If only it could find *him," Josh* said quietly.

CHAPTER 21: Lighting the Way

Emma hosted another movie night for the family. The end credits rolled in muted silence, the flickering light of the TV casting shadows across the room. No one had really said much, but the movie itself hadn't been the focus anyway. It was a way to silently connect. To just be together in the moment. To fill the awkward space they found themselves in.

Josh was the first to leave the living room—once again retreating to private his space. Matt followed close behind sleep on his mind.

Jenna stood up and stretched. She offered to help her mom get Grandpa ready for bed. For once, Emma let her. She welcomed it. Together, they got him changed and settled in to bed for the night. Emma paused and hugged Jenna gently. Grateful for the help.

A homecoming of sorts for the musketeers.

Jenna retreated to take her shower and ready herself for bed. Emma headed to the kitchen to straighten up. Matt was already asleep in his room. He could always fall asleep as soon as his head hit the pillow. How Emma envied that - his superpower.

Dressed in an old soccer tee and shorts, Jenna wrapped her wet hair in towel, turban style. The chill in the air encouraged her to head to the kitchen for a hot chocolate before bed. She padded down the hall in the darkened house. She followed the soft amber glow of the kitchen light above the bar. She was surprised to see her mom sitting there, already sipping hot chocolate.

"I made extra, if you want some," she offered.

"Great minds think alike, Mom. I was coming to make myself some. Do we have any of those crumb cakes left?"

"Sure, in the basket on the counter. Grab me one, too, please."

"I'm glad you're still up, Mom. I wanted to run something by you."

"Sure, Sweetie. What's on your mind? Want to move to the table where it's more comfortable?"

They both settled in the chairs and sipped their mugs of hot chocolate, nibbling on the crumb cakes. They sat in silence for a minute, enjoying the rare moment of peaceful solitude – just *two* of the three musketeers. Emma didn't want to rush Jenna. She let her speak in her own time.

"I've been thinking a lot about Grandma lately. I miss her. She was a big part of our lives. I feel like we've left her in the background with Grandpa taking front stage. I mean, I get it. It's a lot."

Emma nodded slowly. Her fingers curled around the mug, its warmth wrapping her in an embrace. A small tear slid down her face.

"You're right, of course," she sighed softly. She continued, her voice catching in her throat, "We have put her in the background, haven't we?" She cleared her throat. "She was always the steady one. The voice of reason. She was always there, the glue holding us all together. Even when Dad started slipping away. And now…it feels like we've forgotten her. It's not intentional, but it's happened anyway. I miss her so much, Jenna. I do talk to her, but *we* as a family rarely acknowledge her passing. We're wrong for that. I feel so guilty."

"Don't feel guilty, Mom. We all miss her. We *all* let her memory fade. We're just as much to blame as you. Don't carry that burden alone. While there are still two musketeers, she's remains…a silent partner."

Emma sat in stunned silence. When did her little girl get so mature?

"I've been watching you take care of Grandpa – it's hard work, but also pretty amazing You are as strong as Grandma was. *You* may not see it, but I do. I've been on the sidelines mostly. Now, I want to change that. I want to honor your strength. Grandma's strength. I think…" she paused. collecting her thoughts, "I think I want to follow in her footsteps. Maybe that's how I can carry her with me …forever."

***

Emma gazed deeply into Jenna's eyes. She saw some of her own mother reflecting back at her. It comforted her in some small way. A connection she'd missed in her grief. In a rare moment of honesty and openness, Emma leaned into the circle of understanding and trust that Jenna was offering freely.

"I don't feel strong, Jenna. I feel broken. I feel lost. I feel like I'm letting you all down."

"No, Mom. You're not. You *are* strong. You're brave. We see you trying so hard to be there for everyone. We see *you* losing *yourself.* I want to help out more."

Emma felt her wall start to crumble. Stone by stone, not all at once. But it was a start. Jenna was beginning to find her footing in the middle of all the emotional swirl, and Emma was realizing she's not alone in holding the memories anymore. Memories weren't to be clutched to her chest for her alone. Memories were meant to be shared. To breathe life back into her mom.

"When break is over, I want to talk the guidance counselors at school. I want to enroll in the pre-requisite classes for nursing. Get some college credits and get a jump start on it. What do you think? Are you okay with that?"

"I'm okay with that. I'm more than okay."

They both stood up at the same time as if they were using a shared brain. The embrace was deep, meaningful and felt oh so welcome to them

CHAPTER 22: Final Walkthrough

While sad about selling her parents' house, Emma knew it was time to let it go. She asked Josh to help her make one last sweep of the house before the closing. She wanted to engage him more. Draw him out of his seclusion. Let him know, he, too, was seen.

He had his permit now, so she decided to let him drive her there. That certainly sweetened the deal. A promise of dinner at his favorite steakhouse enticed him even more. Josh was never one to pass up a good medium rare steak and loaded baked potato! If he was lucky, he might even get a Brownie Volcano out of the deal.

She opened the door with trepidation. It had been awhile since she'd visited the house. The emptiness was overwhelming. She wandered through the barren rooms, lost in memories. Emma still saw the home as it had been when she was a teen. When her parents were at their best. Mom was still the matriarch. Dad was still, well...*himself*. She sighed deeply.

Being an Army brat, Emma had grown used to moving around every couple of years. Being separated from her dad for long periods of time. She was always having to make new friends because either she moved, or her friends moved. The sacrifices families make are part of military life. What choice was there?

This home, on Pinetree Lane, wasn't where she spent her childhood. That was spent traveling around the globe. It was where her mother finally stopped unpacking boxes. Where they'd settled when Ed retired. A place to finally call their own. She remembered her mother buying curtains, painting the walls any color she chose, planting a flower garden. Hanging pictures without worrying about the nail holes – Army housing hated painted walls and nail holes! It's where she and her parents finally put down roots. They may be shallow roots, but they were her roots.

The house looked ready for the handover. The cleaning team had done a great job of sprucing it up. Fresh paint. Dusted baseboards. Professionally cleaned carpets. The house was ready for a new generation. A new family to create memories as Emma and her family had done.

"Hey, Mom?" Josh asked, joining her in the living room.

"Yes?" Emma replied.

"The garage looks good. Clean. Weird though, not seeing Grandpa's tools hanging on the pegboard. No lawn mower. No workbench. I can't even smell the WD 40 anymore," he added with a hint of nostalgia.

"I know. I feel it in the house, too. It's a clean slate for the new family, but I still feel the shadows of our lives here. Memories flooding in, echoing around the rooms."

"Yeah, sad and happy at the same time. Feels like we're closing a door on our past, Mom."

"We are. A necessary step, I think."

"Has anyone checked the attic?" he asked.

"Oh, gosh, Josh! It never even occurred to me! I don't think so. Can you do that for me?"

"Sure, no problem, Mom - anything for a steak dinner," he replied with a wink.

A wink meant the world to her after the distance that infiltrated their relationship.

***

She followed Josh back to the pristine, organized double car garage. Luckily, there was a drop-down ladder leading to the attic. This was her dad's domain; she hadn't even thought about the attic.

Josh climbed the ladder with more youthful exuberance than Emma would have liked, but she said nothing. She didn't want to ruin this fragile reconnection. Instead, she steadied the ladder.

Josh found a chain for the drop light that hung above his head and pulled it.

Light flooded the attic, and Josh adjusted his eyes to the sudden burst of bright lights so close overhead. He surveyed the attic, finally spotting two boxes in the far corner. He ducked down and walked carefully over the rafters to retrieve them, dragging them back to the opening.

"I found a couple of boxes up here, Mom!" he shouted down. "I'm headed down with the first one, so watch out below."

"I hear you!" And she really meant that in more than just in the context of the moment.

Nearing the middle of the ladder, he passed the first box to his mother and headed back up. They repeated the same actions for the last box. Josh clicked off the light and climbed back down, jumping and bypassing the last few steps. He folded the stairs back up, the sound reverberating through the empty garage as it closed with a loud snap.

"Let's carry these to the car and get that dinner. I'm starving."

Emma laughed, "Josh, when aren't you starving?"

***

As Josh backed out of the driveway, Emma took a final look at the house. It was a real turning point. Closing a chapter of a familiar, well-loved book.

Surprisingly, she felt okay with that.

Jenna and Josh enjoyed their rare moment of being together – just the two of them. It was something they both needed. Their steak dinner was the perfect ending to a great afternoon. Reconnecting felt so good. So overdue. Josh got his Brownie Volcano after all and ate every bite—except for the forkful or two his mom swiped!

CHAPTER 23: When One Door Closes . . .

Following their afternoon of reconnecting, Emma and Josh carried the boxes into the living room, setting them on the coffee table. Emma searched the house for the rest of her family. Josh headed to his room. For once, he didn't feel the need to smoke weed.

She found her dad asleep in the sunroom, resting in the fading light of day on the overstuffed wicker sofa. He seemed so peaceful for a change. His face relaxed. Tension gone.

Matt was seated in a chair going over some work on his laptop. Seeing them there together warmed her heart. Two of the most important men in her life.

"Hey, we're home," she said, quietly. "Where's Jenna?"

"She's in her room. Reading, I think. I got home early and relieved Donna. Thought your dad might use a change of scenery. So here we are."

He looked at her. Proud of the effort she was making to connect with Josh. To start to find *herself* again.

"How sweet," she said, perching herself on the footstool in front of him she continued, "Josh and I had a great afternoon. I think we *really* connected, Matt," she said tucking a stray hair behind her ear. "He seemed his old self today. It was so surreal being back in the old house – empty of our things, only our essence remaining. I was sad at first, then I remembered the old saying, *when one door closes, another one opens*. It's time for a fresh start for all of us."

"Wonderful. Good for both of you. How was dinner?"

"It was nice. Sitting down, eating at my own pace. Josh certainly had his appetite! Not worrying about Dad for a bit was nice. I feel a little guilty about that, though.

"Don't. You needed it. As you can see, Dad is just fine," he grinned. "I make a pretty good sitter, if I do say so myself."

"You do. I'm so grateful to you for that. I know I don't say that enough," she paused, looking at him with respect.

"Josh was so helpful. He even thought to check the attic! It had totally slipped my mind to look up there. I was sure he'd fall through the ceiling, but no worries."

"He can act before thinking sometimes, but I'm glad he was safe about it. I should have thought to look up there sooner. Did he find anything?"

"Actually, he did. Two boxes. I'm not sure what's in them. I thought we could all meet in the living room and find out together."

"Sure, when he wakes up, we'll gather the troops."

Matt set aside his laptop and drew Emma onto his lap. She was startled at first by his quick action, but soon she giggled lightly. Suddenly feeling like a schoolgirl. They sat there in silence. Leaning in to each other. Into the moment. Another connection being remade.

Emma sighed with satisfaction. A small smile spread across her face. Her eyes held a long-absent twinkle as she rested her head on Matt's shoulder. He gently stroked her hair. It felt like they were stepping back in time – to days less complicated.

CHAPTER 24: Unexpected Treasures

Shadows lengthened across the living room floor as Emma adjusted the lamps, bathing the room in warm pools of amber light. Matt was already settled in his favorite armchair; Ed, dozing in and out while he sat in Emma's. She'd asked the twins to join them.

Footsteps echoed softly down the hallway - Jenna, bare feet slapping against the wood; Josh, ever in his sweatpants and hoodie padding along behind his sister. This meeting felt different than the previous one. Less trepidation, more intrigue. They sat down on the couch, flanking their mother.

"Dad, Josh found these boxes of yours in the attic of the old house. Ready to see what's inside?"

Ed's eyes brightened like a kid on Christmas morning. His eyes shifted to the boxes, brow furrowed - a flicker of recognition and confusion.

"Old house, what old house?" Ed asked, perplexed.

Emma gave Ed a gentle smile,

"Never mind, Dad. Let's look inside."

Jenna leaned in, "Can me and Josh open them Mom? Please."

Emma's hands hovered over the dusty boxes, pausing mid-air. She dropped them back into her lap.

"Sure, one for each. Let's see what we find," she said giving them the reins. "Josh, you go first since you found them. Sorry, Jenna. Fair is fair," she laughed. "He did carry them down the ladder."

Josh wiped his hands on his sweatpants and pulled the duct tape off the box closest to him. Peeling back the flaps, he was greeted with a host of military memorabilia.

First he lifted out a folder filled with papers recounting Ed's military career. Next, he found some ribbons and medals.

Reaching in again, Josh pulled out a bag of Army patches from all the divisions his Grandpa had served in. He spilled the brightly colored patches across the table and fanned them out.

"I've been looking all over for those!" her father exclaimed excitedly. He got up from his chair grabbing one eagerly. He looked at Emma and asked, "Gracie, can you sew this on my uniform? I don't want to be out of regulations."

Emma drew in her breath and held it for a moment. It caught her off guard being called by her mother's name. The name coming from her father's mouth pierced her heart, softly like an old lullaby. She barely skipped a beat, though, before answering.

"Of course, I can dear. Can't have you getting in trouble."

Ed patted her hand as she took the patch from him,

"Thank you dear. You always take care of me don't you," he said with a wink and a twinkle in his eye.

The room fell silent.

No one moved.

They all looked at Grandpa – stunned, awestruck, and just a little bit heartbroken.

Returning to his chair, Ed snagged another patch off the table. He sat there quietly turning the patch over and over in his hands, rubbing his fingers against the smooth threads.

***

"There's more," Josh said in the quiet room.

He pulled out a light blue medium-sized case adorned with a golden Roman styled motif. He glanced at his grandfather before slowly opening it. Grandpa gave no hint as to what was inside. The case opened with a slight creak, its hinges rusty, tarnished with age. Inside was a ribbon holding a Silver Star medal. Their eyes went wide, their breath drew in with a small, unified gasp as if choregraphed.

Matt leaned forward reaching for the case. "Is that …?"

"A Silver Star," Emma said, her voice barely above a whisper.

Jenna pointed, "What's that…right there?"

"It's an oak leaf cluster. It means Grandpa earned more than one Silver Star," Matt explained.

"Did you know about this, Mom?" asked Josh.

"No, I never knew. Why would he – and Mom – keep it a secret? There's got to be a story or two here."

Grandpa's previously twinkling eyes dimmed. His face grew sullen, brows drawn together tightly. A fleeting moment of recognition – of *knowing* – crossed his face. He got up once again and grabbed the case from Matt. He stared at the star for a moment then quickly closed the case. The resounding snap startled his family, making them jump collectively.

"Some stories we don't bring home," he said throwing case back in the box.

Ed returned to his seat, pensive and moody.

They looked at one another in silence for a few moments, stealing glances at Ed.

Finally, Josh said, "There's one last thing in here…a flag."

He pulled it out slowly, almost reverently. Its triangle fold still intact. Musty. Faded. The once- white stars yellowed, dulled by age and the quiet ravages of time. Much like Grandpa himself. There was a story in that flag. A memory folded within. Waiting to be discovered. Maybe the papers they'd found would reveal the secrets of the flag.

Grandpa seemed lost in his own world once again. He showed no reaction to the flag. Josh gently placed it back in the box. The gravity of the moment settled over them.

No one spoke.

They simply sat there, soaking it all in.

***

Emma hoped – *they all hoped* – that Jenna's box might bring something lighter.

She stood and gave a soft clap of her hands, ending the stillness.

"Who's ready for some a little intermission?" she asked, looking at Jenna. "Think you could help me grab some iced tea for everyone? Maybe a sugar cookie or two? I know *you* won't refuse, Josh!"

Maybe it was a little too much sugar, but after that tense exchange, they needed a jolt of energy. Jenna nodded eagerly, thankful to have something else to do. By the time Emma and Jenna returned with the snacks, there was a subtle shift in the air. Enthusiasm and curiosity once more filled the room. Grandpa had fallen asleep in the chair. Maybe that was for the best.

Sipping tea and eating cookies, they steeled themselves for the next discovery.

"Ready?" Jenna asked her mom, glancing at the others.

"Now or never, I guess," Emma replied.

"Go for it, Sis."

"I'm fully invested now, Jenna. Go for it."

Jenna's hands hesitated over the box for a split second before curiosity won out.

She struggled to release the tape's strong hold on the box, but soon she had it freed. Carefully she lifted open the flaps and gazed inside.

She found some scraps of paper inside. Pulling them out, she saw they were a child's writing – Emma's scratchings. She glanced at her mom before reading the first one.

The Mouse House

There was a house.
There was mouse.
It was a mouse house.

Emma, age 4

Everyone burst out laughing. Jenna reached inside for another one.

The Christmas Gift

I know something better than a Christmas tree,
Or even the packages just for me.
It is the time when three wise men brought,
A gift for a baby, and a precious thought.
This baby that I tell you of, was God's own Son, His gift of love.
He'd died for all the sins we've done, given to us from God above.
Mary and Joseph were richly blessed,
God chose them because they were best.

Emma, age 6

They all looked at Emma. They didn't even know she liked to write poems.

"Mom," Jenna said, "You were so sweet!"

"I'm not now?!" Emma teased. Then she grew serious. "I can't believe he kept all these. He kept these secretly tucked away like a squirrel hoarding nuts for the winter."

Jenna continued reading.

My Hero

By Emma (age 11)

My hero is my dad. I chose my dad because he is so brave. Last year, my friends and I went ice skating at the pond near my house. Johnny and his little brother Bobby were riding their bikes on the ice. They hit a thin spot and Bobby fell in! We were all screaming for help.

I ran to my house and got my dad. He grabbed a rope with a hook and a blanket, and we ran back to the pond. When we got there, Dad swung the rope like a lasso. When it landed near the Bobby, he told him to wrap it around him and hook it back on the rope. Dad pulled and pulled.

He got Bobby out of the cold water and wrapped him in the blanket. Then he threw the rope again. He hooked the handlebars on the first try and dragged the bike out like it was a big fish he'd caught.

All the kids were cheering. And the grownups that had come there, too. I'm so proud of my dad. He saved a boy from drowning and that's why he's my hero.

Quiet filled the room as they glanced over at Grandpa. He really was a hero.

"I remember that that day," Emma said. "I thought my heart would burst with pride. He was the talk of the neighborhood for weeks after that. The boys' parents insisted on taking us all out to dinner to thank him. We went, but Dad never felt comfortable being called a hero.

"I'll read one or two more before we move on, okay?"

They nodded in agreement. Jenna randomly picked another one and read it aloud.

The Soldier

There was a soldier, strong and brave
Because of this, he's in his grave.
For his country he had fought,
As in the Army he was taught.

He was the bravest of all the rest
And he had many medals pinned on his chest.
He lived in happiness and in war,
And now he roams the Earth no more.
Emma, age 12

They sat there once again, pondering the poem. Ed stirred, half asleep.

"I like that one Emmie. Write Daddy another one." And just like that, he was gone again.

Shock hit them like a ton of bricks. They looked at him, too stunned to speak. That rare moment of lucidity took their breath away. Tears flowed freely down Emma's face. Tears of joy. Tears of sadness. Tears of having lost the Daddy that had once been. Before Vietnam. Before Alzheimer's.

"Here's an old letter, Mom. Can I read it aloud?"

"Okay, Jenna. Go ahead.

My Dearest Gracie,
I am sitting on my cot. I only have a few minutes to write. War isn't for sissies! I've been laying here trying to recall the smell of your perfume. To remember the silky feel of your auburn hair as I twist it in tendrils around my finger. The same fingers that long to stroke your satin skin. I love you, Gracie, and wish that I could be there for the birth of our child. I long to lie next to you and rub your rounded belly and to feel the baby kicking and stirring within you. I want to experience this tiny life we created.

Love,
Ed

"Awkward!, muttered Josh, shifting in his seat. Can we move on to another one, please?"

This was a whole new side of her father that she had never known. Emma grabbed a box of tissues off the end table and dabbed her eyes before Jenna continued reading.

Grandpa stirred in Matt's recliner but remained sleeping. Emma didn't think he would be upset at their reading these stories, learning about him, what memories he held near and dear to his heart. Maybe it wasn't as war-hardened as he thought.

Dearest Gracie,

I got the pictures of Emma today! A daughter, I can't believe we have a tiny little daughter. You say she looks just like you, Gracie, from your ivory skin to your sparkling green eyes and wisps of red hair. Then I know she's the most beautiful baby in the world! I'm so glad she takes after you and not me. How I wish I could be there to cradle her in my arms, to keep her safe. I wish I were there to cradle you in my arms too, Gracie, and tell you how happy and proud I am, but I guess that will have to wait.

Love, Ed

Emma dabbed her eyes. Jenna moved on to read from one of the journals. These were black and white composite notebooks. She read on as he wrote about her first steps…

Dear Emma,

Well, Daddy got home from his first tour in time for your first steps!
You can't believe how happy I was to be able to experience that. I know it was just by chance that your first steps were toward me, but it thrilled me anyway. It was such a big milestone in your young life. I am thankful that I was there to share it with you and your mother.

Dad

her first day at school…

Emma,

Putting you on that school bus today was one of the hardest things
I have ever done. Trudging through the jungles of Vietnam or taking shelter from enemy fire seems a far easier task than letting my tiny little daughter step onto that big yellow school bus. Your mother doesn't know it, but I followed your bus all the way to school just to

be sure you were safe. I love you, little one.
Dad

Other entries talked of her broken arm, her emergency appendectomy. It was there, tucked away. She'd had no idea.

At last, Emma decided they needed to call it a night. It was time to get her dad to bed. They all needed to settle after this emotional day.

Emma's voice softened as she glanced around at her family, her eyes lingering on Ed.

"Opening these boxes reminds me of the treasure hunts Grandpa would send you both on. No map this time. No compass. But there was treasure – real treasure. More precious than gold doubloons or jewels. We found a part of Grandpa that's been lost."

Jenna gave a small, thoughtful nod, a smile tugging at the corners of her lips.

"I never knew he'd done so much."

"Neither did I," Emma said quietly. "But we're finding out now. Maybe that's the real gift here … getting to know the pieces of him we've never seen before."

Matt reached over and squeezed her hand gently, his silent support a balm to her heart.

"We'll keep looking," Emma continued, her voice stronger now. "And maybe, just maybe, we'll find more than we ever imagined."

The family sat there in the warm glow of the lamps, the boxes now closed but the treasures they held, both tangible and emotional, still alive in the room. They'd come closer to each other. And to the man who had shaped so much of their lives; uncovering secrets he'd kept buried for so long.

CHAPTER 25: Threads That Bind Us

Josh took the patches to his room and researched them out of curiosity. Later that week, he slipped into Grandpa's room one late afternoon and sitting on his bed next to the beloved recliner in which Grandpa is sitting. The late day light found its way through the open window, dappling the walls. Light and shadow danced across the room. Curtains fluttered in the breeze.

He shows one or two patches to Grandpa, trying to connect. Trying to understand.

Grandpa took a patch from Josh's hand. He turned it over in his hand, rubbing the threads—the threads that bind him to another place. Another time.

Lucid, just for a few moments, he began to speak. He told of being trapped in a bunker, shots blazing overhead.

***

"I can still smell the earthiness of the bunker's sandbags. Feel the fear – eyes wide open, breath shallow, heart pounding so loudly in my ears it nearly drowns out the gunfire. Almost, but not quite. The screams of my men cut through the din of the gunfire as my men fall - one by one. I was the only survivor. The only one to walk away."

He swallowed hard, "The survivor's guilt …"

***

Ed paused for a moment, then went on,

" I couldn't stand closed-in places after that. Never could work in a damn office. Needed the sky, the air. I needed the sun on my face, working with my hands, to build something after all that tearing down."

He continues on in a quiet whisper,
"I still see their faces – remember their names –Billy Weston. Mark White. James Jackson …"

***

He paused in the middle of talking, his face went blank. His eyes lost their sharpness.
And then – slowly - he faded. Alzheimer's, like a curtain, draws closed again. A quiet, merciful retreat into *not* knowing.

***

This quiet, intimate moment further deepens their connection. Solidifies Josh's decision to join the Army. He feels a deep affection for his grandfather and stares at him, seeing him for the first time as *Ed*, not Grandpa. Realizing there is so much more to his grandfather than he'd ever known. He himself had been yearning to be fully seen but hadn't bothered to truly *see* Grandpa. It humbled him.

Josh no longer sees an old man, ravaged by forgetfulness and confusion. He sees a scared yet brave soldier. A man who risked everything for his family, his beliefs, his country. A man willing to make those sacrifices despite the personal costs. He sees the ghosts of soldiers past. He hears the echoes of their cries – *remember us.*

His heart was heavy. He was proud of his grandfather. Proud of those young men who weren't much older than he is now, fighting in a conflict many never understood. Doing what their country asked of them. Some of them willingly, some not, but all sacrificing their lives. Their peace.

Grandpa slumbers now, peaceful is his recliner. In his unknowing. Josh stands up gathering the patches with a new found reverence. He leans down and gently kissed his grandfather's forehead. He tucked a blanket around the old man and studied the face before him. A face etched like a roadmap of all the places he's been. The things he's seen. The things he's done. The things he's *survived.*

Maybe, in some way, he's earned this forgetting.

Josh quietly left the room, closing the door gently behind him. For the first time since Alzheimer's had entered their lives, Josh felt grateful—for the unexpected peace it brought his grandfather. And he was okay with that.

Back in his room, he glanced at the ROTC paperwork as it sat beside the treasure box. It had been there untouched for days. His guidance counselor had given it to him last week, and he'd tossed it aside, uncertain.

Now, after that moment with Grandpa, he knew. Doubt left him, replaced with conviction – giving him a certainty in the direction his life would take. He felt in control of his own destiny. He felt a oneness with Grandpa. He knew in his heart this is how he wants to honor him –to honor the soldiers whose voices were silenced. The ones that never made it home. He would remember them.

He was resolute in his decision.

Now, to figure out how to tell his parents.

Would they be upset?

Would they understand?

Only one way to find out.

The next morning, Saturday dawned bright and early. There was a tap on his door – the secret rap Jenna used to use when they were kids. She was certainly cheerful this morning, he thought sleepily. On the other side of the door, Jenna announced,

"Time to rise and shine, brother! Dad's got breakfast cooking – ready in five minutes. You snooze you lose – all the more for me!"

Josh stretched, a yawn distorting his face momentarily. He could smell the bacon from here. That was all the motivation he needed. Swinging his legs out of bed, he pulled on his sweats – stomach grumbling loudly. Rubbing the sleep from his eyes, he made his way down the hallway. As he crossed the living room, saw his mom, dad and sister already at the table, waiting for him. He paused, taking in the scene. Even though a teenage boy, his heart skipped a beat at the normalcy of the scene before him. Sheesh, he's getting too mushy, he thought to himself, but a small, crooked little smile flitted across his face.

Dad really went all out this morning – scrambled eggs so light and fluffy, homemade biscuits with butter sliding down the sides, bacon AND sausage. Even hash browns. *Have I died and gone to Heaven*, he thought to himself. This was too good to be true.

He sat down and joined them. Jenna was doing more talking than eating, but that wasn't unusual. He filled his plate with a little of everything. He slathered lots of strawberry jam on his biscuit. He bit in with gusto, red jam dripping off his chin.

Jenna animatedly talked about her CPR course. Her hands gestured wildly as she acted out chest compressions on an invisible patient. About how she felt awkward giving the practice dummy the "kiss of life." Joshed laughed at the image of his sister kissing the dummy.

"Good practice for Junior Prom," he quipped.

***

For a moment, they all resumed eating. He quieted, waited for the right moment to tell them. Jenna suddenly reached across him and stabbed the last sausage patty. For once, she beat him to it. They all laughed.

"That's what you get for being lost in thought. I told you, you snooze, you lose!" she said, making a big show of sinking her teeth into it. "Hmmm, so good!"

"I've been thinking," he started, voice quiet and steady. "About my future. I've finally decided what direction I want to take. I want to join the Junior ROTC at school – go Active Duty after graduation. I want to honor Grandpa like Jenna is with Grandma."

No one spoke right away. He swallowed hard, unsure of their response.

Emma blinked – fork hovering mid-air. A thousand thoughts raced through her mind. As an Army Brat, she understood what all that entailed. *Did he?* she wondered to herself.

Matt leaned back in his chair, thoughtful. He eyed Josh. Was this a passing whim? Rushing a decision based on emotion, duty or obligation? Or was it deeper than that? Jenna thought it was a great idea. She encourage him to tell them more. He looked up.

"I don't want to just wander through life. I want to do something that matters. I want it for myself, not just to honor Grandpa."

"This…," Emma paused. "This is a huge decision. I didn't see that coming, Josh. A brave decision. I'm scared for you, but I know you. You're not one to make rash decisions."

Emma pauses for a moment. She wants to be sure he understands what being a part of the military means.

"Remember Josh, the military isn't just uniforms, ceremonies, traveling the world – it's missed birthdays, tearful goodbyes at the airport, absence from family. It's waiting restlessly for orders to deploy when things heat up—distant conflicts. If you think you are strong enough for all that - if you've truly put some deep thought into this, then I support you one hundred percent."

Matt took a big swig of his coffee before adding,

"I agree with your Mom. And your sister. This could be a great opportunity for you. A way to learn a new skill, a career. A chance to get an education. To travel. To learn about other cultures. Then I have to say, I'm onboard, too. If this is what you really want, I suggest you try out the ROTC. See if it's what you think it is. If it feels like a good fit over the next two years, then I'm all for it."

Josh released a gentle sigh. That went better than he thought. He felt a peace inside. He felt seen. He felt heard…for the first time in a long time.

Emma's phone dinged. According to the camera app, Ed was stirring in his room. Time to start the day. Josh released a gentle sigh. He felt a peace inside. He felt seen. He felt heard…for the first time in a long while.

CHAPTER 26: A Gentle Reprieve

Matt had sat on the sidelines, offering quiet strength where he could - but in passive ways.

He'd been watching Emma slowly fade away; a dull, faded copy of herself. He couldn't— no, he *wouldn't* - let that continue. Unable to save herself, it was time for him to act – to be fully vested in fulfilling the wedding vows: *for better or for worse, in sickness and in health.* He'd meant those words all those years ago, and now it was time to follow through.

He picked up his phone and made an appointment at a day spa for her. Then, he arranged for respite care, ensuring Ed would be looked after, and allowing Emma a much-needed break. He hoped a soothing massage would be just the thing she needed to begin letting go.

He walked into the kitchen where he found Emma sitting at the bar sipping a coffee.

"Hey, Em. I have a surprise for you," he said as he took the stool next to her.

"A surprise? I don't know if I can handle any surprises right now, Matt."

"I think you'll like this one. You have an appointment tomorrow at 10 a.m. at *Solace & Tranquility Day Spa* on Main Street. You know the place? It's got great reviews. I think it'll be just what you need – a good, long, deep massage to help you relax."

"But I …" Emma began. "I have to …"

Matt interrupted gently,

"You have to take care of *yourself*, Em. You're no good to anyone if you collapse from exhaustion. I checked your calendar on the fridge for conflicts, and Donna has agreed to watch Ed. No excuses."

Emma looked at him, softening.

"How did I get so lucky to have you in my life?" she asked.

"It wasn't luck," he said with a grin. "I pursued you endlessly, if you recall."

"Tonight, after work, George is coming over to visit. He said he'd watch your dad so we can go out to eat as a family. It's been far too long since we've done that. You get to pick the restaurant. George is more than capable. He *wants* to help, let him. And, because I'm such a great guy," he said with that boyish smirk, "here's some money to go pick out a new outfit, too."

Emma had to admit it. She needed this break. She had felt herself cracking lately, pieces of her splintering off. And here was Matt, silently picking up the shattered pieces and fitting them back in place. He wasn't trying to fix her - just remind her she was still intact. Still worthy of love.

***

Emma entered the small changing room at spa with some trepidation. She'd never spoiled herself like this before and she was unsure of what to expect. Still, she had to admit, it felt good to have a little bit of time for herself. She pushed back the guilt - it was counter-productive to the purpose of the spa.

She shed her clothes, wrapping herself in the robe provided –white, soft, fluffy – like a cloud surrounding her, hiding her. She slipped her tired feet into a pair of slippers lined up against the wall like dutiful soldiers. Sara, her massage therapist tapped gently on the door.

"Ready, Emma?"

"Ready as ever, I guess," she replied.

Sara led her to the massage room.

"Lay down on your stomach, nestle your face in this cradle. I'll cover your hips with a heated towel."

Emma was grateful for that. She was feeling a little too exposed. Too vulnerable.

Sara asked, "Do you have a music preference? Meditative, white-noise, brown-noise?"

"Meditative, please."

"Good choice."

Dimming the lights, Sara oiled her hands, rubbing them together to warm them.

"Have you had a massage before, Emma?" she asked, pretty sure of the answer.

"No, never. My husband surprised me with this. I have to admit, I'm a little nervous,"

"No worries, Emma. I'll explain every move before I make it. That way you know what's coming."

"Sounds good," Emma replied, closing her eyes.

The scent of chamomile and lavender filled her nostrils, soft and soothing - like a warm hug. The lavender reminded her of her mom. Gracie always did love flowers.

"Okay, Emma, I'm going to start with your neck and shoulders, ready?"

As Sara started, she felt Emma's tension – tight and knotted. She began a deep massage. Gentle, yet firm.

"I'm going to go with a therapeutic massage if that's okay with you, Emma. It's a little more pressure, but necessary to release these knots."

Emma mumbled a quiet okay, her face buried in the padded rest, cradling her like the comforting hands of her mother.

She could feel the Sara's skilled, knowledgeable fingers firmly easing the tension from her body as she worked her way down Emma's back, her thighs, legs and lastly her feet.

Emma relaxed, dozing in and out. Thoughts drifting to better days. She hadn't felt this rested in a very long time. She may have to make a habit of this.

"Okay, Emma. Now, I'm going to use some heated basalt stones and oil to glide over your spine from your lower back to your neck. Then, I will put new ones to sit there for a few minutes. Ready?"

"Mm hmm," Emma answered in a low, contented voice.

The heat sank deep into her muscles, far more natural and comforting than the artificial warmth of a heating pad. She felt the tension as it seeped out of her like water flowing across a riverbed.

Oh, Matt, you knew just what I needed she thought herself as she left *Solace & Tranquility Day Spa*. She almost felt like she was her old self. Almost. Her body and her spirit renewed, if only for a little while.

***

Birdsong Boutique sat just next door, its window display catching her eye. Why not go in and spend the rest of Matt's gift? After all, he'd insisted. She browsed the boutique, lingering - touching different fabrics, feeling the textures and enjoying the colors that popped out at her. Finally, her fingers settled on the perfect outfit.

If one looked closely while she exited the store, they might even think they glimpsed a skip in her step.

***

The restaurant Emma chose was *Vecchia Vita* (Old Life*)*. A quaint little Mom and Pop Italian place the kids used to love - back when eating out was cherished weekly ritual. It was tucked in a quiet, secluded part of town. Safe, familiar. Inviting.

Seated at a corner booth near the back, the ambiance wasn't lost on Emma. The red-and-white checkered tablecloths, straw-covered Chianti bottles - candle wax dripping down the sides like a waterfall. Hand painted murals of the Italian countryside, shelves sporting old wine bottles, copper pots and garlic braids hung from hooks. It felt like stepping back in time or into an old movie scene. It brought warmth and comfort. They had been coming here for years. It was good to be back there as a family again.

***

Later that evening, lying in bed, nestled against Matt, Emma reflected on the quiet comfort of the day. She realized how much she'd miss the last couple of years. It refilled her spiritual cup as much as Marco had filled her wine glass. A brief step back from her responsibilities … a gentle reprieve. Little did Emma know that reprieve would be as fleeting as it was precious.

CHAPTER 27: Storm Clouds Gather

It started simply. Barely noticeable at first. A mere blip on the radar.

Dad began refusing to eat. Sometimes he'd shove his plate off the table, flinging food on the floor. Other times he'd squint at her suspiciously accusing her of trying to poison him. Not even his favorite dishes tempted him anymore.

She tried everything. Milkshakes made with Strawberry Ensure - he used to love milkshakes. It worked for a while. A few sips here and there. She took it as a small win.

And always a cough, getting worse over the month. Slow. Subtle. A summer cold, maybe? It dragged on, a dry, constant cough. No sneezing, no runny nose, no fever. Just that endless cough echoing through the house.

***

"What are you doing - cooking it with pennies?!" he snapped one day, pushing his plate away.

Emma blinked, startled by the oddity of it.

Pennies?

What an odd thing to say.

She scraped yet another plate of food down the garbage disposal and wiped the table in silence. She'd been chalking his behavior up to Alzheimer's, but now she began to wonder. Could it be more?

Shelby, one of the respite caregivers, came in to the kitchen as she arrived to start her shift.

Emma glanced at her.

"Shelby, you know how hard it's been getting Dad to eat. Now, he thinks we're putting pennies in his food when we cook it! Have you ever heard of such a thing?"

Shelby paused, setting her bag down on the counter. She was thoughtful for minute.

"Actually … yes," she said slowly, carefully, not wanting to overstep her bounds.

"It's called dysgeusia. It's when people experience changes in taste - usually a metallic taste. Like copper. Or *pennies*."

***

Emma straightened, her exhaustion forgotten. Her interest piqued.

"Is it a symptom of something?" Jenna asked hesitantly.

Shelby hesitated, being very careful with her words.

"I think there may being more going on here. Especially combined with that dry cough he's had. I'm not a doctor, but …" She looked at Emma gently. "Sometimes those are signs of lung cancer."

Emma froze. Her chest tightened, her breath caught. Her mind everywhere and nowhere all at once.

"I can call and to set up a doctor appointment if that helps," Shelby offered softly.

Emma nodded, feeling light headed. Shelby noticed and pulled out a chair for her. She brought Emma a cool glass of water.

"Here - sip it slowly. *Breathe*."

Outside, a summer storm was brewing.

Inside, emotional thunderclouds ended the gentle reprieve with a resounding clap.

Shelby gave her a gentle squeeze on the shoulder.

"Will you be okay? I need to check on your dad."

Emma gave a slow nod.

***

She didn't know how long she sat there. It seemed like an eternity. The front door creaked open, and Matt stepped inside. Before he could close the door, a few leaves swirled across the threshold settling in the entryway, driven by a sudden gust of wind.

"Hey, Em? I brought –"

He stopped in the kitchen doorway. The sight of Emma sitting at the table, her arms circling her head gently as she rested it there.

"Emma?"

She raised her head. Weariness engulfed her like fire out of control. Her eyes were red, her face tear-stained.

He closed the gap, quickly reaching her. He pulled her up towards him. He held her in a tight bearhug. Unsure what had happened. Giving her space to let him in when she was ready.

Emma leaned deep into him, burying her face in his chest. His embrace welcomed her. She had fit so perfectly there. In her safe space for nearly 25 years. His timing had been perfect.

My anchor, she thought to herself. Always my anchor when I need him. God knows she had needed him so much the last couple of years – now more than ever.

"I'm here," he whispered gently. "When you're ready – I'm here."

***

They stayed like that for a moment or two.

The sounds of the storm raged outside. Flashes of lightning. Cracks of thunder. Echoing the internal storm in Emma. She leaned deeper into him, trying to absorb into him. To disappear.

"It's Dad. Shelby thinks he…" her voice hitched, but she continued. "She thinks…he might have lung cancer."

Matt led Emma gently to the living room, sitting her on the couch beside him.

"Tell me, Emma. Tell me why she thinks that."

And so she did. Words suddenly spilling from her like the rain flowing out of a drain spout.

"One day at time, Emma. Let's take it one day at time," soothed Matt.

She nodded. Grateful for this man sitting in front of her. For his strength, his love, his understanding.

"No matter where this part of the journey takes us, Emma, I'm here. The kids are here. We're in this together. You are not alone."

As the storm outside calmed, so did Emma – for now.

She wearily rested her head on Matt's shoulder, eyes tracing the streaks of rain sliding down the window. Somewhere in the distance, a final rumble rolled across the sky – low and steady. The storm outside was moving on.

For Emma, the storm was just beginning.

CHAPTER 28: Collateral Damage

It wasn't the enemy that marked him in the end.

Not shrapnel. Not gunfire. But something far more insidious – a slow betrayal by the very country he swore to protect.

When all the tests were done, the diagnosis was definitive: lung cancer. The most likely cause? Agent Orange.

A chemical herbicide used by the US military to strip the jungle foliage bare, to flush out the enemy, to make them easier targets. But the enemy weren't the only ones hiding in the jungle foliage. American soldiers engaged the enemy, manned the camps, drove the supply convoys. Breathed in the same air as the enemy.

Emma's exhaustion, both physical and mental, was taking its toll. She was bitter, angry, disillusioned. *Had no one thought of that? Had the powers that be decided that was an acceptable risk? It wasn't their necks on the line. It wasn't their sacrifice.*

Agent Orange - such a *clean, fresh* sounding name. But there was nothing clean or fresh about this parting gift. It felt more like a delayed ambush. A final shot fired long after the cease-fire.

Like napalm burning slowly, insidiously through everything it touched.

Collateral damage. That's what they were. Emma saw it clearly now. Her family was a victim of the fallout – making sacrifices they never signed up for.

Medicare and Tricare paid for his healthcare. Ed would ultimately pay with his life.

CHAPTER 29: The Weight of Truth

The twins were nervous. They knew something was wrong. They felt the undercurrent of tension in the air – had seen the lines of worry etched on their mother's face, the frequent fleeting glances between Emma and Matt. Not the warm looks of romance, but something else entirely - concern, unease, a silent shared communication of two people shouldering a weight of truth too heavy for words. Emma's eyes often vacant, drifting off somewhere far away, lost in a place none of them could reach.

So they weren't surprised when they once again found themselves sitting in the sunroom for a family meeting.

But this one felt different. Heavier. No one wanted to be there yet here they sat.

Emma wished – deeply, achingly – that she didn't have to pull the kids into this. That she could shield them from this burden. But she'd tried that already. And it had nearly broken her.

Josh and Jenna deserved the truth, much as Emma wished she could shield them from it. The last year and half - losing their grandmother, adjusting to living with their grandfather and his Alzheimer's - had forced them to grow up too soon. To help carry a weight they shouldn't have to bear. And now, she was adding more.

She took a deep breath, hoping the openness of the room and the sunlight streaming through the windows might ease the gravity of her words, the tightness in her chest. By sheer force of will, she began to speak, her voice carefully controlled – or so she hoped.

Matt held her hand in his, gently squeezing it.

A silent promise: *I'm still here, you are not alone in this.*

And so, the dark, heavy words of truth spilled from her in a slow, quiet and measured voice.

"Grandpa is sick," Emma began, her eyes fixed on a loose thread of the blanket Jenna had drawn across her knees in an almost protective mode. "It's more than Alzheimer's...it's his lungs."

***

The room went still, only the sounds of indrawn breaths by Josh and Jenna.

The twins sat silently, unmoving, stoic – hunched over like gargoyles atop an ancient building. Their eyes drilling into Emma wanting to know and yet not wanting to hear the heavy truth they felt was coming.

Emma swallowed hard.

"There's a cancer growing there…and it can't be removed – or even cured. It's too late for chemo or radiation. We didn't know he had it, and it has spread too far, too fast."

Jenna moved to the couch, edging closer to Emma. Needing a connection. Needing grounding. Like Emma, needing an anchor in this sea of uncertainty. She took Emma's other hand and clung to it tightly while resting her head on Emma's shoulder. Tears brimming in her eyes and gently sliding down her cheeks. With her other hand, she wiped them away.

"We're calling in Hospice to help care for Grandpa around the clock. They'll be giving him strong medication to control pain. We're going to keep Grandpa here, make him as comfortable as possible. He'll have us all here with him, loving him through it. That's what matters now."

"I wish this didn't have to happen, Mom. To him … to us. It isn't fair," she whispered.

"I do, too, Sweetie. It's almost too much to bear."

Josh remained silent, processing. He wasn't trying to avoid his feelings, or to be manly. He was just numb. He didn't know what to feel.

"How," Jenna paused, "how long until…you know?" she asked quietly.

***

The question hung in air like the hush after a lullaby, echoing in the stillness of the room. Matt broke the silence.

"The doctor says maybe three to six months. Hard to say for sure. I know it's going to be hard over these next few months. We're going to get knocked down sometimes. That's just life. But we've made it through a lot already. And we'll make it through this, too—together."

Josh nodded, almost imperceptibly, eyes glistening with unshed tears. He didn't want to cry. Not in front of them. He kissed his mother's head, rested a hand on Matt's shoulder—not just for balance, but for something solid to hold onto—and then slipped out of the sunroom. He hadn't smoked weed in weeks. But today? Today, it felt justified.

Jenna, too, rose to retreat to her room. She needed time to process this alone.

***

Matt asked, "Emma, you good?"

"Yes. Thanks for always being there. I won the lottery with you. I'm grateful."

"I'm proud of you, Em. You did as good as you could - given the news."

"I'm going to sit here a bit longer. Feel the sun on me. Think or maybe try *not* to think," she laughed without humor.

Matt left saying, "Call me if you need me. I'll be in the office."

Emma curled up on the outdoor sofa, staring out the window. Silence wrapped around her like a heavy quilt. She looked out at the hydrangea bush. There sat a cardinal, seeming to stare back at her. Another of Gracie's favorites.

Emma smiled through the stinging tears that once more spilled out. That small flash of red warmed her. Mom was still there. Watching. Bringing her comfort. *Be the calm in the storm, Emma.*

She closed her eyes and fell asleep, a much needed reprieve.

CHAPTER 30: Quiet Goodbyes

Acceptance was hard, but necessary. Moving forward was vital to their survival. Each one handling the news differently. Acceptance came to each in their own time. But for Ed - time was running out, though he was unaware of his inevitable demise. Alzheimer's keeping him cocooned, protected him. Death would slip in unexpectedly. Without dread or fear. Silently luring Ed away from his family. From his trauma.

***

Donna and Shelby still came two days a week to allow Emma time for herself. Time to breathe. Time to prepare herself mentally as best she could. Hospice was called in. They provided a hospital bed, full-time nursing, with morphine to ease his pain. Certified Nursing Aides came three times a week to bathe him. Hospice care is often hard to understand, it's goal to make the patient comfortable, to ease the transition from the now to the hereafter. Vastly different from traditional medicine whose goal is to cure, to heal. The nurses did their best to help the families they assisted to understand this difference.

***

Jenna came to Grandpa's room every day after school. She'd sit beside him, perched on the bed as she read to him, combed his thick, white hair, and trimmed his nails. She even watched *Gunsmoke* with him. Sometimes she'd read aloud from his favorite books, eager to help, content to just be near him. To simply exist in this space with him. She shadowed the nurses, wanting to learn firsthand all that she could. They didn't mind. They saw her compassion, how quickly she learned. She'd be a great nurse.

***

Josh brought in his desk chair and each evening he'd sit quietly by Ed's side. He could've sat in Grandpa's recliner, but it felt wrong. It was *his* chair. He'd talk to Grandpa, tell him stories of his favorite memories of time spent together. Sometimes, Grandpa seemed to be listening – a faint smile flickering across his face. He wasn't sure, but he hoped he heard him.

***

The morphine made him sleep and, in that sleep, memories were given voice. They rose from his grandfather unbidden. He'd speak, almost as if awake.

His words were clear, not mumbled as he relived tales of Vietnam: radioing in coordinates for evacuation, giving orders to his men, asking for his compass and map to plot their course. He'd laugh at the antics of JoJo, the monkey who had befriended the soldiers in the camp, often stealing things from them. Sometimes his voice was firm. Other times it trembled in fear or concern. Occasionally, a laugh escaped his lips, but those moments were rare. More often, his face would twist and contort to match the scene unfolding in mind.

Josh would quietly reach out, gently hold his hand, and murmur softly that it was just a dream. It was unnerving, but he showed bravery and understanding beyond his years. It didn't dissuade him from his decision to join the military, though. If anything, it strengthened it.

***

The twins had the evening hours with Grandpa, and Emma the days. That left Matt the early morning hours before work. The night nurse would slip out to give report, allowing Matt his privacy.

***

Ed was usually asleep at this early hour, but that didn't stop Matt from making these final connections. He and Ed had always gotten along. Matt's father had died when he was a child, and Ed had taken on a fatherly role, mentoring Matt. Teaching him how to be a father.

***

The soft glow of a nightlight was the only source of light, softening the mood a little. Giving it a reverence.

***

"Hey, Ed," he said softly, his voice low and steady. "It's Matt."

***

There was no reaction. He hadn't expected one. Ed would occasionally cough or moan, stirring slightly in the bed before resuming his slumber.

***

"I want you to know much you mean to me – and to say thank you." He laughed to himself, "I don't think I've ever said that to you. Here's another first – I love you, Ed."

***

He paused, as emotion choked him.

***

"Thank you for letting me marry Emma. For showing me what being a husband looks like. For your constant support and encouragement. For setting me straight when I needed it."

***

Another pause,

“ For showing me how to work on a car or fix a washing machine. You weren’t a big conversationalist, but I understand now. I get it. But you showed up. Did what needed doing. I’m grateful for that.”

***

Matt shifted his weight, and took Ed’s hand, squeezing it gently, not expecting a return squeeze. Just a need to connect.

***

“She’s tired, Ed,” he whispered. “Emma’s tired. But she’s still fighting for you. Still loving you through all of this. And I’m trying my best to love her through it, too. To be strong. I’m trying to take a page from your book.” Silence wrapped around them - not awkwardly, but warmly, like an old blanket. He sat there a little longer, still holding Ed’s hand. Listening to Ed’s labored breathing. As he moved to leave, he felt a gentle squeeze back. It may not have been intentional, but he’d take it.

***

Matt placed a hand on Ed’s frail, now bony shoulder and gave him a gentle pat.

***

"Rest easy, old man," he murmured. "I promise I'll take care of her for you."

***

Emma lowered the bed rail, sitting quietly beside her father. The nurse had opened the curtains allowing the soft mid-morning light to flow in. This was her time, the house quiet with everyone at work or school. The nurse in the kitchen organizing the meds. The steady noisy puffs, hisses and hums of the oxygen machine were the only sounds she heard. Its white-noise filling the otherwise silent room.

***

She held his hand, intertwining their fingers. With her other hand, she gently stroked the back of his hand, turning it to notice the paper-thin skin - dry and flaking. She traced the blue veins that stood out against his pale skin, like highways marked on a road map. The nurse slipped in quietly and swiftly injected his meds.

***

"I'm sorry, Emma. I need to turn him on his side. We don't' want to irritate that bed sore." Emma got up, allowing her to do her work. When the nurse left the room, Emma resumed her spot next to Ed.

***

"It's me, Daddy. It's Emma. Oh, Daddy, I hate this for you. It's so unfair." Her voice, deep with emotion, caught in her throat. Her chest tightened, and tears spilled down her cheeks.

"I'm not going anywhere. Daddy. I promise."

***

No response. Just the uneven rise and fall of his chest, now sunken.

She smiled weakly, brushing a bit of hair from his forehead.

***

"I won't leave you, Daddy, not ever."

She lay down gently next to him, her hand sitting lightly on his shoulder.

***

"They say you don't understand what's happening to you, but you can probably hear us. Maybe that's true, maybe not. I'd like to think you can."

***

Memories spilled from her, flowing freely as water across the smooth stones of a stream.

***

"Hey, Daddy. Remember the time you taught me to ride my bike? You held on as tight to the back of the banana seat as I did to the stingray handlebars of that sassy purple bike. You ran alongside me for what felt forever. I kept begging *Don' t let go, Daddy!* You promised you wouldn't. But you did. And suddenly I was speeding along on my own. I was so wobbly, weaving down the street dodging parked cars. I remember turning and realizing you had let go. I was so happy with myself, I forgot to be mad at you for letting go. I was flying along on my bike because of you, Dad. You let me take my solo flight even though letting go was scary for both of us."

***

Emma paused. Lost in memories.

***

"Or that time at the cabin when you let me steer the boat when I was 10 and I nearly ran it ashore? Those poor ducks took flight as the sight of me driving zigzag around the lake. I was afraid of getting too far from shore. You gently took my hands in yours and helped me regain control of the wheel, laughingly telling me you were getting dizzy from my driving."

She lay there silently next to her dad for another moment.

***

“And my wedding day…” she added, smiling, eyes still closed as she snuggle next to him. “You were so handsome in your Army dress blues, medals on your chest, black shoes shined to perfection. You stood so tall and proud, silently giving me your strength. When it was time to walk me down the aisle, you took my hand and whispered, ‘*Don’t rush. We’ve got time’.* And in that moment, I wasn’t nervous anymore. You gave me assurance - confidence in my decision to marry Matt. Thank you, Daddy for always making me feel safe. Protected. You may have officially given me away to Matt, but I always knew you would be there by my side supporting me. Supporting us.”

***

“I know you’re tired, Daddy. Tired of being strong. Tired of forgetting. Missing Mom.”

***

Again, emotion paused her.

***

“It’s okay, Daddy. You were a good husband to Mom. You did your best to be a good Dad. I know now why you could often be distant and moody - and it’s okay. I get it. You deserve release from the demons that haunt you. I promise you I’ll be okay. Matt will make sure of that. He’s strong. He’ll carry me through this.

The kids will be okay, too – they're resilient, tough like their Grandpa. If you're ready to go – to take this final solo ride, I understand. I'll let go of you and let you fly high. I give you my blessing."

***

Still no response.

She lay there next to him, watching him struggle to breathe.

The hum of the oxygen machine lulled her to sleep, nestled next to Ed.

***

The nurse crept in to check on them. Glancing at them lying there, she is reminded why she does this job. She quietly covered them with a blanket and slipped from the room, leaving Emma alone with her father. Had anyone been there, they'd have noticed a tear or two slipping from her eyes. This job was tough and emotional, but oh, so worth it for moments like these. Dark moments of death on the horizon simply reaffirming the essence of life.

CHAPTER 31: A Reunion with Gracie

Days came and went, blending together like the fading colors of sunset. Emma spent more and more time sitting with her dad, soaking up these moments like a sponge. Trying to lend him her strength and her drawing strength from him in an almost symbiotic manner. Their routines continued daily like clockwork – like a changing of the guard.

Some mornings, Ed surprised Emma with a rare moment of clarity, sharing a memory with her. He'd reach for her hand, and mistaking her for Gracie, stroke her cheek. Once, only once, he looked at her and softly, smiled and whispered, "*My Emma*."

She liked to open the window and let in the light and fresh air to chase the shadows of death away. When he was awake, Ed would often glance outside as if expecting someone before the morphine once again drew him into slumber and restless dreams. She wished she could ease those nightmares.

Emma watched him sleep as she knitted absently, needles clicking in the relative silence of the room. Nurses came and went, tending to his needs and checking on Emma. Time crawled on. Life marched on…at least for now.

***

One day as Emma dozed in Ed's recliner, Gracie appeared before her.

I wasn't sure if I should come yet. If the time was right, but I miss him so. I'm proud of you, Emma. You kept your promise to me. I'm grateful to you. I'm so proud of you. You did your job. Your task is almost complete. Soon, your dad and I will be reunited. Be strong, sweet daughter. I love you.

Emma jolted awake, sweat pouring from every pore, goose bumps dotting her cool flesh. She looked around the room anxiously for her mother, calling out to her. It took her a moment to realize her mother wasn't there. It was a dream. No, it was more real than that. It was a visitation.

She leaned back into the recliner, heart pounding, tears flowing. Closing her eyes again, she tried to slow her breathing, to still the thoughts racing through her. Her mother had come to prepare her.

***

Matt entered the room and immediately noticed Emma's face, a reflection of shock and wonder at once. His eyes darted to Ed and back to Emma. He crossed the room quickly, placing a steady hand on her arm. Her eyes flew open.

"I saw her, Matt! My mother - she came to me. I *saw* her!" she burst from the recliner.

Matt pull her into an embrace, then gently held her at arm's length, searching her face.

"Em, what are you talking about? I'm confused. Explain it to me."

And so she did.

He stood quietly as her words sank in, his eyes never leaving her. Understanding took root.

"It's almost ending, isn't it, Matt?"

"I think so, Em. I don't know for sure. But yeah…I think your mom was easing you into it."

***

The nurse returned to check on Ed. Matt took Emma to the living room to take a break. They sat together on the couch in the unusual quiet of the afternoon, snuggled together for strength and comfort. Emma dozed in the strong warmth of her husband's arms. With her head on his chest, the gentle, rhythmic thumping of his heart soon lulled her into much-needed sleep. Matt held her with one arm and stroked her hair with the other.

Later that evening, the nurse came into the living room with soft urgency in her voice. She told

Emma she'd heard the telltale sound – the death rattle. She explained it was the final stage of the dying process.

Matt left to get the twins and explain what was happening. They had known this was coming, but even so it felt like a shock – the dreaded moment had arrived at last. Both unwelcome and unavoidable.

Together, they entered the room. At their request, the nurse waited outside the room. The family gathered in somber silence, circling Ed's bed. Emma grabbed one of his hands, and Jenna the other. Matt stood beside Emma, one hand at the small of her back, supporting her physically and emotionally. Josh stood next to Jenna unashamedly holding her hand.

They clung to one another as they whispered their love to Ed, one voice at a time.

***

Then, though it shouldn't have been possible, Ed's eyes fluttered open. He looked upward, a faint smile on his face.

"Gracie," he whispered, barely audible.

His chest rose and fell. Rose …fell …

And then rose no more.

Tears filled their eyes. Grief welled in their hearts.

Gracie and Ed - reunited at last.

CHAPTER 32: A Hero's Farewell

The house lay in silence.

Not the kind of quiet that comes when the kids were at school, Emma and Matt at work or running errands. Not even the hush of late nights when the only sound heard is the soft hum of the refrigerator or Matt rhythmic snoring from their bedroom.

This silence was different.

A stillness that almost echoed, deafening even in its silence.

Not peaceful, not gentle - but cloying and heavy, pressing itself into the furthest corners of the rooms. It filled the air like a dense fog, unwelcome and unrelenting.

Emma sat at the kitchen table that her father had built with his own two hands. A wedding gift to them many years ago. She rubbed her fingers against the smooth, satin-finished oak. It was so much more than just a kitchen table. It had been home to family dinners, birthday cakes, pizza boxes, games nights, homework,

and late night last-minute school projects. Now it held folders full of her father's documents and a growing list of phone calls to be made and funeral to-do lists.
Emma picked up the blue and white death certificate and felt the raised seal that made the document official – not that she needed it to know it was true.

When they had found the treasure boxes in the attic, Emma had put all Ed's Army documents in a fireproof safe. Rummaging through it now, she found Ed's **DD-214**, the discharge papers every veteran learned to protect. She passed it across the table to the man sitting opposite her.

***

George Smithers, her father's oldest friend, and Army brother, accepted it with same care he might have once reserved for handling a fire arm. He hadn't hesitated when Emma asked for help navigating the process of arranging Ed's burial at *Arlington National Cemetery***.** Ed's *Silver Star* had earned him the right to military honors on that sacred ground.

"George, I don't know what I'd do without your help," Emma said softly. This whole process is just … it's so overwhelming. So many steps."

"It's the government, Emma," he said with a dry half-smile. "Red tape's a part of the package. But I'm glad to help you. My friend deserves to be buried there - caisson, Taps, the whole nine yards."

"Mom's ashes … her urn will be placed above his casket, like they always planned?" She asked as she let out a breath she didn't even know she was holding.

"Absolutely," George said, "Her urn will be buried above his casket. Both names will be on the headstone, but remember, his information goes on the front of the headstone and your mom's will be on the back. That's just protocol. Buried together, just like they always wanted."

He'd known Emma since she was a young child. George reached across the table and took her hands in his.

"No worries, Emma. We'll make it happen. Just takes a lot of paperwork and phone calls to Arlington and the funeral home to get things lined up. We will be assigned a civilian representative from Arlington to assist you. You tell me when you know more and I'll come right over and help you."

***

Two days later, Emma stood at the bay window of the kitchen. Her hands wrapped tightly around Ed's favorite coffee mug. She slowly sipped the too-hot, too-strong coffee, gazing out the window without really seeing. Her vision turned inward with the past and the present blending together. Memories running endlessly through her mind like music on repeat.

She could clearly see her parents sitting in their living room of their old home - Ed in his recliner, working a crossword puzzle, and Gracie in her armchair, crochet hook in hand, a lap full of yarn.

She could see him sitting there, chewing the tip of the pen as he thought. Removing it before asking,

"Gracie, what's a seven letter word meaning skip a stone across the surface of the water?"

Without a second thought, she answered, "Dapping."

"You always know the answers, Gracie. Where'd I be without you?"

"I'll never give you the chance to find out!"

The memory warmed her. Then the chirping trill of her cell phone sounded, jerking her back to reality. Her heart skipped a beat at the unfamiliar number.

"Hello?"

"May I speak to Mrs. Emma Roberts, please?" asked the disembodied voice.

"Yes…yes, that's me. Thanks so much for calling," she answered, voice shaking with barely controlled emotion, chest tightening.

"This is Mark Reyes with the Arlington Cemetery. I'm calling in regard to your father's burial arrangements. Let me begin by offering my most heartfelt condolences. We are grateful for your father's service."

"Thank you."

Reyes spoke respectfully and efficiently, confirming Ed's eligibility for military honors at Arlington. He went over the final checklist: dates, preferred funeral home, transportation for the remains to Virginia, and the verification of his service medals – including the well-earned Silver Star.

Emma, tears wetting her cheeks again, grabbed a pen and note pad, scribbling notes with in her shaky grip as he spoke.

"Okay, ma'am, we will be in touch. Is there anything else that I can assist you with?"

"No, thank you so much. We'll be waiting for your call with the rest of the details. Thank you again for your help."

When the call ended, Emma slid into the seat at the kitchen table, thoughts scattering like grains of sand in a dust storm. She glanced at the empty chair across from her – Ed's chair – occupied only a couple of days ago by George.

Reaching for her cell phone once more, she texted him a simple message:

I just heard from Arlington. They are ironing out the detail and will be in touch soon. Thanks again for all your help, I'd be lost without you, George.

Almost immediately, his reply dinged back:

Always. I've got you, kiddo. We'll get him there, Emma. He deserves this honor. I've contacted our unit. Some of the guys are hoping to make it to the service. We owe Ed that much.

She pressed her phone to her chest, closing her eyes. For the first time since her father's passing, she felt the faintest shift in the air – a thread of momentum. Not closure, not yet. That would hopefully come at Arlington. But motion, a way forward.

***

Emma, Matt and the twins arrived by limousine to the cemetery and entered Arlington's Memorial Chapel. George and the others followed close behind.

The chapel was quiet, an unnatural hush that carried the weight of the service about to unfold.

They walked down the aisle and took their reserved seats. Emma sat in the front pew, Matt closely by her side. Jenna was by her mother's side, and Josh by his father. The polished wood of the well-worn pews reminded Emma of the lovingly crafted kitchen table Ed had made. The scent of the polished wood pews, and numerous flower arrangements standing at attention near the casket filled her nostrils. Sunlight filtered through high arched stained glass windows, casting colorful shades of light across the floor. Emma stared at the banner of her father's image beside his coffin. The sounds of guests finding their seats, murmuring quietly to one another in greeting. Some coming to offer condolences to Emma and her family, others choosing to leave them in sorrow, afraid to approach.

A solemn reverence filled the room as the Army chaplain made his way to the pulpit, his uniform neatly pressed, Bible in hand. A unified hush fell on the chapel in anticipation. His voice was low and grounded, as he spoke not just of death, but of a life of service, dedication and sacrifice – of a life that had made an impact not just on Ed and family, but the nation at large. He read Psalm 23, his voice steady as a rock, followed by a prayer that settled like a warm blanket offering comfort to the chill Emma felt inside. Emma bowed her head, not out of habit, but out of love. The chaplain invited George to the pulpit.

Then came the stories, some solemn, stoic and reverent, but others light-hearted - balancing the mood delicately. One by one, Ed's brothers-in-arms made their way to the pulpit to share their connection to Ed. For even in the deep loss of death, life lives on – in the stories, the memories, and the unyielding connections. Emma and her family were overwhelmed at the outpouring of love these men had for Ed. Men they had never met, but who had shared the worst times of their lives with him. There were tears and there was laughter. There was sorrow and there was joy.

And then George returned to the pulpit.

His hands trembled slightly, the paper in his hand soft and creased from his nervous folding and unfolding. But when he spoke, his voice was sure and steady, tinged with great respect for his old friend.

"Ed McAllister wasn't just a soldier. He was an anchor to all who met needed him. They guy who would cover your post so you could get a moment or two or rest. The one who we all knew we could count on in wartime and after. He was our friend. He was our brother. He will not be forgotten, even when the last of our unit is gone."

George paused, wiping an errant tear from his eye.

"I'm Lt. Colonel Smithers. Colonel Edward McAllister always upheld military traditions. We do this Final Roll Call to honor him.

"Sound off for roll call,"

George raises his voice somewhat loudly and begins the time-honored ritual of deleting a deceased service member from the roll. As the names are read, each member of Ed's unit stands up, responds, and returns to sitting:

Sergeant Mitchell.

George waits for a response.

"Present, Master Sargeant."

Staff Sargeant Smith.

George waits for a response.

"Present, Master Sargeant."

Major Johnson.

"Present, Master Sargeant."

Colonel Edward McAllister.

Three seconds of silence.

Colonel Edward McAllister.

Three seconds of silence.

Colonel Edward McAllister.

Three seconds of silence.

George's breath caught for a moment.

"Colonel Edward McAllister is missing from the roll."

Major Johnson stands and replies, **"Strike Colonel Edward McAllister from the roll."**

George steps away from the podium and sits down as the Bugler plays **Taps**.

***

Emma pressed a hand to heart as the following silence filled the room, deep and holy. She could feel Ed's absence – vast and undeniable – but also his presence, like a steadying hand at her back. There wasn't a single dry in the chapel as they sat in reverent stillness, the weight of emotion washing over them like the waters of baptism.

***

Emma and the family filtered out of the chapel closely followed by the brothers-in-arms and the other guests. They waited for the procession to begin.

The U.S. Army's 3rd Infantry Regiment - the Old Guard - loaded the casket to the caisson with dignity and precision. A sacred representation – of the nation, of all who served, and all who mourn.

Outside, the sunlight had softened, and a light breeze stirred the leaves in little eddies, nature seeming to pay her respects, echoing the reverence of the moment. The caisson, now holding the flag-draped casket, was led by six white horses, their leather harnesses gleaming, their hooves steadily clacking on the sacred path leading to the cemetery.

The honor guard followed behind the caisson with rifles shouldered, backs ramrod straight, arms to their side with white-gloved fists held tight as was protocol. The slow, measured cadence of the military escort set the tone as the procession led the long walk to the gravesite.

Matt took Emma's hand in his and Jenna's in his other. Josh stood next to his mother taking her other hand - together, a unified family. The others followed closely behind. Along the walk, visitors to the cemetery yielded to the procession, conversations hushed, hands to their hearts, or snapped salutes by fellow service members. The procession wound its way along the paved path to Ed's final resting place. It comforted Emma, knowing her mother would be inurned with him, together forever.

***

Each white marble tombstone they passed reminded Emma that she was not alone in her grief. Thousands upon thousands had walked this same path – literally and figuratively. She was also comforted that her dad was surrounded by men and women, though not known to him, who had similar experiences.

When they arrived, they stood together as the casket was removed with ceremony and care. The honor guard moved in practiced unison, placing the casket atop the polished metal stand before the open grave. Emma's breath caught in her throat as she took her seat, her heart pounding. The others stood at a respectful distance, still as statues.

The chaplain approached once more. He offered a final prayer, his words calling forth comfort and courage, weaving Scripture with gratitude. Emma barely registered the words. Matt placed his arm around her shoulders as he, too, wiped a tear unashamedly from his face. Josh and Jenna sitting almost as rigid as the honor guard themselves. Seeing Josh in his Army Junior ROTC cadet dress uniform, filled Emma with pride. Josh hoped Grandpa would be proud of him.

***

Then came the seven soldiers with the three volleys salute:

CRACK.

CRACK.

CRACK.

Each shot rang out across the open space, piercing and precise. Emma flinched at each volley, feeling the sound as it reverberate through her.

The haunting notes of a trumpet followed. Each note of "**Taps**" rising and falling slowly, echoing through the nearby trees that also stood at attention. Mother nature once again giving nod to the solemnity of the moment. The sounds of the trumpet made the music feel like a prayer. Emma was trying hard to hold it together, failing miserably.

***

They watched the honor guard approach the casket and in a silent, ritual act, fold the flag unified, precise. Snapping it expertly as they went. The sound reverberating around them. The presenting officer approaches Emma:

"On behalf of the President of the United States, the United States Army, and a grateful nation, please accept this flag as a symbol of our appreciation for your loved one's honorable and faithful service."

The silence of the presentation of the flag still lingering, reverent and thick, as George approaches the family and glances at Emma who gives the smallest of nods.

***

George steps over to Josh.

The boy – *no, young man* –sat tall in his ROTC uniform, eyes red but shoulders squared.

George reached into the inner pocket of his coat, pulling out a small blue box that carried within it its weight and history. Josh instantly recognized the case from the box he'd discovered in the attic. Josh rises to meet George, back straight, hands in proper fists at his side.

George didn't say a word at first. Instead, stood before Josh, swearing a loyalty to him much as he'd done years ago to Josh's grandfather.

George opens the box.

Inside, the Silver Star gleams, its brilliance undiminished by time. Its meaning even more poignant in this setting.

"Josh, your grandfather earned this in a place most men would've run from, but not Ed," George said quietly, voice cracking with emotion. "He ran in full force, for me and the rest of the men in our unit. He tucked it away in the attic, never fully feeling that he deserved it. But me and the other men here from our unit know he absolutely earned it. We were there."

He held the medal out to Josh.

"Your mom wants you to have it. To carry his courage and bravery forward."

Josh swallowing hard, accepts the medal with trembling fingers – praying he won't drop it.

"I'll make him proud, sir," he chokes out.

George places his hand on Josh's shoulder giving it a gentle squeeze.

"You already have, son, you already have. And I'm offering you my support, such as it is. I'd be honored to serve as your mentor in his place."

Josh rose and like the man he was becoming, he shook George's hand firmly.

They all rose and approach the casket. They lay flowers across it smooth, highly varnished wooden top giving their silent farewells.

A daughter's farewell. A grandchild's farewell. A soldier's farewell.

"Rest easy, Daddy. Tell Mom I said hello."

CHAPTER 33: Life Full Circle

Emma sat on the swing on the screened-in porch of the cabin her father had left her. She and Matt had retired here six years ago after giving Jenna and her husband their home. They'd never regretted the move. She sipped her coffee and looked out across the mountains cloaked in spring foliage. Matt was cooking them breakfast before they headed to the airport, her stomach rumbling in anticipation.

***

He joined her on the porch.

"Breakfast is ready, Em," he said, dropping a kiss on top her head.

"It smells good. Let's grab the plates and eat out here and watch the sunrise," she said, starting to rise from the swing.

He put his hand out, halting her.

"I'll get them, you sit. I'll be right back. Want any orange juice?"

"No, thanks. I'm good with coffee."

They sat in silence watching as the sun rose to bring light and promise to this day. Finally, she rose and grabbed the plates.

"I'll wash these real quick while you load the car, okay?"

"You got it, babe"

***

They had a safe flight dozing as they made their way to Washington, DC. Once they retrieved their luggage from the spinning, shiny carousel, they ordered an **Uber** to take them to the hotel where the twins were waiting. They were the last to arrive.

***

"First time in DC?" asked the **Uber** driver.

"No, we've been here a few times. But this time, our grandkids will be here, too."

"Always nice to have family around. It's supposed to be good weather this week. Hope you get out and enjoy the sights. The cherry trees are in blossom. You should check them out. Here we are."

***

Emma and Matt checked in and group texted Josh and Jenna to say that they'd arrived.

"I can't wait to see them. I'm so excited. It's been a while," Emma told Matt excitedly.

And with that, there was a knock at their door.

***

She practically ran to open it, trying to beat Matt. She won.

She swung the door open and there was Josh. So tall and handsome, blond hair in regulation cut, dressed in jeans and a polo top. Right behind him was Jenna and her husband David. Peeking between them were their four year old twins.

"Granny! Pops!" they cried in unison, pushing past the others. They ran to Emma and Matt, eager for hugs and kisses.

"Did you bring us anything?" they asked excitedly. Emma never missed a chance to get them something no matter how small.

Their greetings over, they settled into the room and visited a while.

David said, "I'll take the kids down to the pool while you guys catch up. You can't do that with two crazies running around. They can rest before we go to dinner. What do you say, Jen?"

"Be good for Daddy, and you might just earn dessert after dinner tonight."

Again in unison, "We will Mommy! Bye Granny and Pops!"

The room quiet once again. Josh told them about where he might get stationed next. He was excited it might be Japan. Emma, now had a BSN in

Nursing, told them of her job at the Veterans nursing home where she worked two days a week. Matt and Emma told of their recent adventures of their trip to Ireland.

Then the topic came around to the true reason of this family reunion – the anniversary of Ed's passing. The burial at Arlington.

***

"I can't believe it's been 10 years," Emma said. "So much has happened since then. At the time, I didn't think I'd get past all the heartache. We've all come a long way. Finding our happy places at last."

"We were worried about you, Mom. But you dug deep and reached out. I'm grateful that you finally let us in," Jenna said in a quiet voice.

Matt chimed in, "We feared we'd lose you, too, Em."

"I know, and I'm so sorry for that. I'm thankful for all of you for noticing – for saving me. I'm eternally grateful."

***

"Well, let's lighten the mood here, where are we eating dinner? I'm starving!" said Josh.

They all laughed, then Emma said, "When aren't you hungry, Josh? Some things never change. You choose, but keep in mind the kiddos – they are addicted to chicken nuggets."

***

The next day dawned with blue skies filled with clouds as white as cotton balls, no rain, and plenty of sunshine. After breakfast at the hotel restaurant, they took a couple of **Ubers** to Arlington. There they retraced their steps to the gravesite of Ed and Gracie. This time their hearts were less heavy, filled with hope and promise. Emma traced the carving of her parents' names in the stone, cool and strong beneath her fingertips as she told them of all the changes in their lives.

With the children getting restless, it was time to say goodbye – for now.

Emma lingered behind as her family walked slowly ahead of her. The air ached with reverence. Watching them depart, her heart swelled with pride. She shifted her gaze to the carefully manicured green lawns, and the budding trees pushing forth their Spring blossoms with the promise of new life.

***

Every direction Emma looked was dotted with white stone markers standing at attention, tall and proud as the men and women they represented. Some residing in their final resting place with their spouse beside them, others in lonely solitude in their eternal slumber. All resting at-ease in a well-deserved peace. A nation grateful for their service and sacrifice.

She glanced once more at her parents' headstone and was reminded of the sacrifices they, too, had made for the sake of country and family. She was grateful for having found her peace at last. Proud she and her children carried on those legacies they'd left behind for Jenna and Josh, and for Jenna's twins, their namesakes: little Gracie and Ed. Her parents' hopes and dreams now marching into the future.

A new generation carrying forward their legacies.

Acknowledgments

I want to thank my family for their unwavering support and patience. Your love and understanding carried me through the darkest and most difficult parts of this journey, and for that, I will always be grateful. This book is for you.

To my parents, Bob and Mary, who taught me how to love, and to respect others. For showing me how to live a life of service, dedication, and faith. I miss you both but parts of you live on within this novel, and this book is for you.

To my sisters Shelley and Rebecca, who listened to my ramblings, joys and frustrations throughout my life. For sharing our grief and loss of our parents. For always being there for me—this book is for you.

To my children, Alex, Jake, Zachary and Katilyn, who have taught me more about love, strength and resilience than I ever knew I had. This book is for you.

For my grandchildren, Coraline, Jack, Eleanor and Lemi, for giving me such love and joy and making me feel young again in spirit, this book is for you.

A special thank you to those who shared their experiences of caregiving, grief, and love with me.

Your stories inspired this book and gave it heart, this book is for you.

To anyone who has ever cared for a loved one through Alzheimer's or any other illness: your strength, courage, and sacrifices are reflected in every page of this book. May you find comfort in knowing you are not alone, This book is for you.

Lastly, to all the US service men and women, and to those buried at Arlington and other National Cemeteries, this book is to honor your service and sacrifice. I thank you. This book is for you.

With love and gratitude, thank you for walking this journey with me.

Additional Resources for Support

For those navigating grief, Alzheimer's caregiving, or hospice care, the following organizations may offer support, guidance, and helpful information:

- **Alzheimer's Association**
  Website: www.alz.org
  National Helpline: 1-800-272-3900
  The Alzheimer's Association provides resources for caregivers, education on Alzheimer's disease and related dementias, and support groups for individuals and families affected by dementia.

- **National Hospice and Palliative Care Organization**
  Website: www.nhpco.org
  Find a hospice provider near you and learn more about palliative care options. The NHPCO is dedicated to advancing care for individuals with serious illnesses and supporting caregivers.

- **GriefShare**
  Website: www.griefshare.org
  GriefShare offers a network of grief support groups for those who have lost a loved one. Their programs provide comfort and healing to those in mourning.

- **National Alliance for Caregiving**
  Website: www.caregiving.org
  The National Alliance for Caregiving provides resources for family caregivers, including guides on managing caregiving responsibilities and accessing community-based services.

Disclaimer: The resources listed above are for informational purposes only. Please consult with professionals to determine the most appropriate support for your individual needs.

About the Author

Beth Gribas is a writer, storyteller, and empath who draws deeply from her own life experiences to craft emotionally resonant narratives. Born in 1960 and raised as an Army brat, Beth spent much of her childhood moving from place to place, which gave her a unique perspective on the world and an ability to connect with others from all walks of life. This rich tapestry of experiences, combined with her deep roots in her Scottish and Irish heritage, influences much of her writing.

Beth's writing reflects the love and connection she shares with her family. She is the proud mother of three sons, two of whom have followed in the footsteps of their grandfather by joining the military. Beth's father, a career Army officer, had a significant impact on her children's lives, shaping their sense of duty, honor, and service.

But perhaps the most profound influence on Beth's life is the love she shares with her four grandchildren. They are the light of her life, and she treasures every moment spent teaching, guiding, and playing with them. Her writing is often inspired by the joy and love they bring into her world.

Beth's first novel, *Legacies,* is a deeply personal exploration of family dynamics, caregiving, grief, and the emotional challenges of living with Alzheimer's. The story centers around Emma, a woman struggling to balance the needs of her family with the demands of caring for her father, who is slowly losing his memory to dementia. In Emma's journey, Beth explores the universal themes of love, loss, and the resilience of the human spirit.

When not writing, Beth enjoys spending time with her grandchildren, volunteering in her community, and exploring her heritage. She is a passionate advocate for the Alzheimer's Association and other organizations that provide support for families affected by dementia. Beth continues to write, with plans for future novels that explore more of her family's rich history and the power of storytelling to heal and connect.

For more information on Beth's work, visit **www.amazon.com/author/bethgribas.** You may also follow her on Facebook at **Beth Gribas, Author.**

www.ingramcontent.com/pod-product-compliance
Lightning Source LLC
Chambersburg PA
CBHW050335110726
47899CB00007B/2510

* 9 7 9 8 9 9 8 8 1 4 5 3 2 *